Born in Hertfordshire, England, on 29 May 1952, Louise Cooper describes herself as 'a typical scatter-brained Gemini'. She spent most of her school years writing stories when she should have been concentrating on lessons, and her first fantasy novel, *The Book of Paradox*, was published in 1973, when she was just twenty years old. Since then she has published more than sixty books for adults and children.

Louise now lives in Cornwall with her husband, Cas Sandall, and their deaf white cat. When she isn't writing, she enjoys singing (and playing various instruments), cooking, gardening, 'messing about on the beach' and – just to make sure she keeps busy – is also treasurer of her local Royal National Lifeboat Institution branch.

Visit Louise at her own web site at www.louisecooper.com.

Louise Cooper

PUFFIN BOOKS

PUFFIN BOOKS

Published by the Penguin Group
Penguin Books Ltd, 80 Strand, London WC2R 0RL, England
Penguin Putnam Inc., 375 Hudson Street, New York, New York 10014, USA
Penguin Books Australia Ltd, 250 Camberwell Road, Camberwell, Victoria 3124, Australia
Penguin Books Canada Ltd, 10 Alcorn Avenue, Toronto, Ontario, Canada M4V 3B2
Penguin Books India (P) Ltd, 11 Community Centre, Panchsheel Park, New Delhi – 110 017, India
Penguin Books (NZ) Ltd, Cnr Rosedale and Airborne Roads, Albany, Auckland, New Zealand
Penguin Books (South Africa) (Pty) Ltd, 24 Sturdee Avenue, Rosebank 2196, South Africa

Penguin Books Ltd, Registered Offices: 80 Strand, London WC2R 0RL, England

www.penguin.com

First published 2003
1

The moral right of the author has been asserted

Set in Adobe Sabon
Typeset by Rowland Phototypesetting Ltd, Bury St Edmunds, Suffolk

Made and printed in England by Clays Ltd, St Ives plc

British Library Cataloguing in Publication Data
A CIP catalogue record for this book is available from the British Library

ISBN 0–141–31439–7

This book is dedicated to all the staff and pupils of St Agnes School in Cornwall, who eagerly encouraged me to write it – and will doubtless find the setting familiar!

chapter one

Dad said, 'Nearly there,' and Tamzin Weston's heart sank into her shoes. She looked out of the car window at the little Cornish village they were driving through, and thought how bleak everything looked – as bleak as she felt.

She desperately wanted to say, 'Please, Dad, please, I don't want to be here!' but she bit the words back. She knew that Dad and Mum had to go abroad because of work. She also knew why she couldn't go with them. They would be travelling all over Canada, living mostly in hotels, which would make things like school impossible. Tamzin was trying to understand, but it would be a whole year before her parents came home again. And meanwhile she must stay with her nan – Dad's mother – in an isolated house in a place that she had never seen before. It made her feel very dismal and more than a little scared.

It wouldn't have been so bad if she really knew Nan. But they hadn't met since Tamzin was about five, and Tamzin could hardly remember her. They sent each other Christmas and birthday cards and presents, but Nan hadn't been to visit them for years. She was an artist, and Dad joked that she was a bit eccentric. She looked nice in photographs but what sort of person was she really? Tamzin couldn't help wondering if maybe Nan didn't like children. It would explain why she had hardly ever come to visit, and the thought worried Tamzin. If it was true, how on earth were they going to get on?

Well, she would soon find out. They had left

the village behind, and now they were driving along a narrow lane with rough, plant-covered stone walls – Dad said they were called Cornish hedges – on either side. Then the lane turned, and ahead of them was a deep valley that led towards the sea, with cliffs rising on either side. Down a steep hill, then Dad turned the car on to a rough track that led off the road, and a minute later Tamzin saw Chapel Cottage for the first time.

The house stood on its own in a small garden surrounded by scrub and gorse. It was built of grey stone, and in the dull October afternoon it looked chilly and unwelcoming. They bumped down the last stretch of track and stopped next to a little yellow car that was parked outside the house. As Dad switched the engine off, the house's front door opened and Nan appeared.

She was tall, with black hair piled up on her head, and she was wearing baggy old trousers and a loose top that was splashed with paint stains. Her skin was very tanned, and she was smiling. They got out of the car and Nan kissed Dad. 'Peter!' she said, then turned to Tamzin. 'Hello, Tamzin, dear. It's a long time since we last met, isn't it?'

Tamzin nodded. 'Yes . . . Nan.'

'You must be tired after the journey,' Nan continued, 'so come and have some tea before we see about your luggage.'

She led Dad into the house, still talking, and Tamzin trailed after them. They entered the kitchen, which was enormous and very old-fashioned, with a low ceiling that made it dark and gloomy. A fluffy black cat was curled on a chair. Tamzin held out a hand but the cat jumped down and walked away, which didn't make her feel any better.

She sat at the big wooden table while Nan poured tea. Dad was talking about Canada, and Tamzin tried not to listen. She was on the verge of tears already and the conversation only made her feel worse. So to distract herself, she looked around the kitchen – and had a pleasant surprise.

There was a painting of a horse on the wall, several china horses on the shelves, and a row of polished horse brasses hanging from one of the beams. Tamzin's spirits lifted a little. Her biggest dream was to learn to ride and, maybe, have a pony of her own one day.

Nan saw her looking. 'Do you like horses?' she asked.

'I love them!' said Tamzin.

'She certainly does,' Dad agreed. 'She's always wanted to have riding lessons but there aren't any riding schools near us.'

'Oh, it's very different here,' said Nan. 'In fact there's a riding stable just up the valley.' She smiled at Tamzin. 'I'll show you in a day or two, when you've settled in.'

'There,' said Dad, teasing. 'Before you know where you are, you won't be missing Mum and me at all!'

That wasn't true, of course. Tamzin was

going to miss them dreadfully, and her friends, and everything she knew. But maybe life at Chapel Cottage wouldn't be so bad. For Dad's sake, anyway, she was determined to put on a brave face.

'Don't worry, Dad,' she said, and managed to smile back at him. 'I'm going to be fine. Really I am.'

Tamzin's new bedroom overlooked the valley. It was a nice room with a comfortable bed, wardrobe, dressing table and even a wash-basin of her own. She couldn't glimpse the sea from the window but Nan said that the beach was only a short walk away, down the valley path.

There was another horse picture in her room. It was in a similar style to the one in the kitchen, and when she looked at it closely Tamzin saw Nan's name signed in the corner. These paintings were hers, then. They were very good, Tamzin thought. And all very blue:

blue skies, blue light – this one was a moonlit picture of a horse with a flying mane and tail, galloping out of a blue sea. The horse was white, but its coat had a blue tinge . . . Nan must have a thing about blue, Tamzin told herself, and smiled.

Nan came in behind her, carrying one of her cases. 'What do you think of my pictures?' she asked.

Tamzin turned round. 'They're lovely! Especially this one – I think I like it the best.' She looked at the picture again. 'Do you always paint horses?'

'Nearly always,' said Nan. 'Though I sometimes do other things to sell. I used to ride, you know, but I wasn't very good at it. So now I just do horse pictures and collect a few horsy things.'

Tamzin smiled shyly at her. 'Thank you for putting this one in my room. It'll be the first thing I see when I wake up every morning.'

* * *

Nan's expression changed. 'The first thing you see . . .' she mused. 'Mmm . . . that's probably just as well.'

Whatever did she mean? Tamzin wondered. Nan's face was thoughtful, and there was a peculiar little downward curve to her mouth, as if she was worried about something. But before Tamzin could ask any questions, she seemed to shake her thoughts off and was suddenly brisk and cheerful.

'Dinner's nearly ready, so hurry and unpack, then come down. I'll see you in a few minutes, all right?'

She went out, leaving Tamzin mystified.

After dinner the three of them settled in the sitting room, but before long Tamzin began to feel miserable again. Dad was staying overnight but in the morning he would drive back home, then the day after that he and Mum would board their plane and fly away to Canada. It was all looming horribly close.

Tamzin hated being weak, but if she wasn't careful she would start to cry.

Nan saw her blinking and looked kindly at her. 'This must be very dull for you, Tamzin,' she said. 'Why don't you go and explore the house, and leave your dad and me to chat?'

She understood without the need to be told, and Tamzin accepted gratefully. If nothing else, it would take her mind off her troubles.

Chapel Cottage wasn't that big but it was certainly interesting. There seemed to be lots of little rooms, with twisty passages and steps leading to and from them. You couldn't exactly get lost but it was easy to pretend you could. And in every room Tamzin found, there were more of Nan's horse paintings. Most of them were quite small but a few were as large as the one in her bedroom. Again, the paintings and the horses in them were all very blue.

The last room she came to was Nan's

studio. It was at one end of the house and it had huge picture windows on three sides, almost like a conservatory. It was dark now, and long curtains were drawn over the windows, but there must be a marvellous view in the daytime.

The room was full of canvases, tubes of paint, rags and bottles; all the clutter of an artist's workplace. There were two half-finished paintings on easels, one a portrait of two children, the other a blue sea-and-sky scene. Blue again . . . Was Nan going to add a horse to that picture? Tamzin wondered.

She moved slowly round the room, looking at everything but being careful not to touch. In one corner stood a tall cupboard with a glass door. She paused in front of it, to see what was inside – and stopped.

On a shelf in the cupboard, roughly level with her eyes, was a little statue of a horse. It seemed to be made of a kind of rough stone, and in the shadows away from the ceiling light its colour looked granite-grey. The horse was rearing high and, though it was quite crudely carved, it somehow seemed so realistic that Tamzin shuddered. Everything about it was *angry*, from its stiff mane and tail to its teeth, which were bared in a ferocious challenge. Chips of red stone had been set into the skull to make its eyes, and they glittered in the gloom with a strange, cruel light of their own.

Tamzin stood motionless, staring. The statue fascinated her, yet at the same time there was something frightening and horrible about it. Part of her wanted to run out of the room and never look at it again. Another part, though, was urging her to open the cupboard door, reach in and pick the statue up. It was as if the angry little horse was calling to her, hypnotizing her.

'Tamzin?'

Tamzin spun round as the spell shattered. She felt strangely guilty when she saw Nan standing in the doorway and, confused, she babbled, 'I'm sorry! I was only looking, I wasn't going to touch it!'

'Touch what?' said Nan.

Tamzin gulped. 'The statue. The one of the rearing horse.'

'Oh,' said Nan. 'You've seen that, have you?'

Tamzin nodded. 'It's . . . creepy,' she said.

'It's that, all right.' Nan's face was suddenly grim. 'And it's very old. It's been in the family for centuries. I keep it there out of the way because . . .'

Nan hesitated, and Tamzin ventured, 'Because it's so valuable?'

'Yes,' Nan agreed quickly. 'Yes, that's it. It's very valuable and it mustn't get broken. So I want you to promise me that you won't touch it.'

Tamzin nodded. 'I promise.'

'Cross your heart?'

Tamzin was surprised. Adults didn't usually

12

say things like that, but from the look on Nan's face it was clear that a simple promise wasn't enough. She was waiting, and uneasily Tamzin nodded again. 'Cross my heart,' she repeated solemnly.

'Good.' Nan looked relieved. 'Well, it's getting late; time you were in bed. Would you like some hot milk before you go?'

She was deliberately changing the subject, and suddenly Tamzin knew that what she'd said about the statue wasn't the whole truth. There was another reason why the little horse was kept out of the way, and Nan didn't want Tamzin to know what that reason was. Suddenly Tamzin wanted to know. She *wanted* to very badly, and she started to say, 'Nan, why is the statue –'

Nan interrupted. 'Never mind that now, dear.' Her words were kind enough but her voice was sharp. 'I said it's bedtime. Come along.' Then she hurried Tamzin out of the room and shut the door very firmly.

* * *

As they walked away, Tamzin looked back. She felt uneasy, and she didn't know why —but she didn't like the feeling at all.

chapter two

Tamzin woke up in the dead of night. She had been dreaming about the little horse statue and, though she couldn't remember the dream clearly, she was sure that there had been something frightening about it.

She tried to go back to sleep. But she couldn't stop thinking about the little stone figure, and suddenly she felt angry. Why had Nan made her promise not to touch it? She wasn't going to drop the statue and break it; she was old enough to be responsible, and much too careful to do anything silly. It was *insulting*. What right did Nan have to tell her

what she could and couldn't do? If she wanted
to touch the statue, why shouldn't she?

It wasn't at all like Tamzin to get so angry
about such a petty thing. But it didn't occur to
her that there was anything strange about the
feeling. Eventually she did manage to sleep
again, but the last thought she had before her
mind drifted away was: *I'll touch it if I want
to. I will. I will.*

She woke in the morning to the sound of gulls
screaming as they wheeled above the house
and along the valley. The day was bright, with
a brisk wind; the air smelled fresh and salty,
and from the garden it was just possible to
hear the sea. Even the black cat (who was
called Baggins) was friendly and purred at her.
But Tamzin hardly noticed all these things.
She was thinking about the little stone horse.

At breakfast she was very quiet. Dad was
leaving soon, and he and Nan thought that her
silence was due to misery. They would have

been surprised if they'd known the truth.
For Tamzin was hardly thinking about Dad
at all.

She was still thinking about the little stone
horse.

Dad hugged her before he drove away.
'Cheer up, poppet,' he said. 'The time'll fly by,
you wait and see. Be strong – and try to have
some fun.'

'Don't worry, Peter, I'll take good care of
her,' said Nan. 'Phone us when you get home,
won't you?'

'Of course I will. And we'll ring again
tomorrow, before we leave for the airport.'

Tamzin kissed Dad goodbye and watched
until his car disappeared from sight along the
track. Tears welled in her eyes, making the
garden and the valley blurry. She rubbed them
away then went back into the house.

'All right?' Nan, who was in the kitchen,
asked kindly.

Tamzin nodded. 'Yes. Thank you.'

'I'm going to the village soon. Would you like to come?'

Tamzin's heart gave a strange, eager skip. 'Um . . . do you mind if I don't?' she said. 'I'd rather go to my room for a bit.'

'Of course. I understand. Tomorrow, maybe.'

Tamzin almost ran upstairs, and when she reached her room she shut the door and sat down on the bed. She felt breathless and excited. Nan was going out, which meant that she would have the house to herself for a while.

And down below in the studio, the little stone horse was luring her . . .

A few minutes later Nan called out to say goodbye. Tamzin heard the bang of the front door, then the sound of Nan's yellow car starting up and driving off. She waited until the noise of the engine had died away in the distance, then she stood up and ventured out on to the landing. Her heart was jumping like a grasshopper, and she had a strong urge to go on tiptoe down the stairs. How silly – there was no one to hear her. Yet she couldn't shake off the feeling that another, unseen presence was in the house, following invisibly in her footsteps.

In the hall, the sense of being watched was so strong that she looked back over her shoulder. It was just her imagination, of course. There was no one there. Baggins was asleep on a kitchen chair and took no notice as Tamzin hurried to Nan's studio.

Nan had obviously been in here this morning, for the curtains at the picture windows were pulled back. The view was wonderful but Tamzin ignored it. She went to the corner cupboard and looked through the glass door.

The stone horse was still there. She had been half afraid that Nan might have moved it, but it seemed Nan trusted her to keep her promise. Tamzin felt a pang of guilt. Deep down she knew it was wrong of her to break her word. Then the guilt faded. What harm could there be in just holding the stone horse for a minute? She would look at it more closely then put it carefully back, and Nan would never know that she had touched it.

The cupboard door wasn't locked but it was very stiff, as if it hadn't been opened for a long time. When Tamzin finally managed to jerk it open, the whole cupboard rocked. The little horse teetered too, then suddenly it tipped right over.

'Oh, no!' Tamzin made a desperate grab for the statue as it started to fall from its shelf. For one awful moment she thought it was going to slip through her fingers and crash to the floor, but at the last instant her hands seemed to close of their own accord, and the statue was safely caught. She breathed a vast sigh of relief then, as her pulse slowed down after the panic, she looked closely at her prize.

The horse *was* made of a granite-grey stone,

and it wasn't at all beautiful. In fact, she thought, it was ugly, with its heavy head, ears laid flat back and savage expression. It looked . . . what? Tamzin fumbled for the word she wanted and found it at last. It looked *cruel*.

She turned the statue over and saw that some words had been carved on its base.

'*Gweetho An Men Ma* . . .' She murmured them to herself. Whatever did they mean? They were not like any language she had ever seen, and she could make no sense of them.

A cold shiver went through Tamzin. Something about the stone horse was making her skin crawl. Why had she been fascinated with it, so fascinated that she had been ready to break her promise to Nan? All those feelings had suddenly winked away into nothing, leaving a sense of dread in their place. She didn't want to touch the statue any more. She didn't want anything to do with it. She just wanted to put it back and try to forget that she had ever set eyes on it.

She turned quickly back to the cupboard, stretching up to the shelf – and the stone horse moved in her grasp.

Tamzin gave a cry of shock, and jerked her hands up. She didn't mean to fling the statue away from her but she couldn't help it. In an awful frozen moment she saw it spinning in the air, and she knew what was going to happen.

The statue hit the floor and shattered into pieces. As it broke, Tamzin had a second shock – for a chilly light flickered through the room and she seemed to hear an eerie, bell-like sound that was almost like a horse neighing shrilly. She stood frozen, staring down in horror at the smashed statue. The light and the sound had gone in an instant but she was certain she hadn't imagined them. What did they mean? *What had she done?*

Desperately she dropped to a crouch and

started to scrabble for the broken fragments,
trying to gather them all up. There were so
many; she'd never find them all, she'd never –

'Tamzin?'

The voice came from the doorway.
Alarmed, Tamzin looked up. She hadn't heard
the car returning, but Nan was there. She was
standing very still and her face had turned
pale.

'I . . .' Tamzin swallowed. 'I didn't mean
to . . . I was holding it and it seemed to *move*,
and . . .'

Nan took a deep breath, then she exploded.
'You stupid, disobedient girl!' she shouted.
'What did I tell you about the statue?'

'I'm sorry!' Tamzin pleaded.

'What's the use of being sorry? It's broken!
Oh, you fool, you wretched, meddling little
fool!' In two strides Nan was across the floor.
Tamzin thought she was going to grab her arm
and shake her, but she didn't. Instead she knelt
down and started frantically to collect more

fragments. 'Help me!' she snarled. 'Pick them up! All of them. Make sure you get every single one!'

Almost in tears, Tamzin did as she was told. She was as frightened by Nan as she had been by the weird incident. But Nan didn't shout at her again. Instead, a stormy silence hung over the room as the two of them gathered up the pieces of the stone horse. Trying to make amends, Tamzin looked under furniture and crawled into corners until at last she was certain that every fragment must have been found.

'All right,' Nan replied curtly when Tamzin said she'd found them all. Then abruptly Nan's shoulders slumped. 'Oh Tamzin, I'm sorry I shouted at you. I didn't mean to. It was just the shock.'

Tamzin bit her lip. 'It was my fault, Nan. You told me not to touch it.'

'Yes, I did.' Nan sighed. 'Look, I think it would be best if you went out for a little

* * *

while. Walk down to the beach for an hour
and leave me to finish clearing up. We'll both
feel better by then.'

Tamzin didn't want to go anywhere but
she was too shaken and ashamed of herself to
argue. She hadn't seen the beach yet, and
maybe some sea air would help to calm her
down. Certainly it seemed like a good idea to
stay out of Nan's way for a while.

Nan was still on her knees, searching the
floor as if she didn't trust Tamzin to have
found all the broken pieces. At the door
Tamzin opened her mouth to try to apologize
again. But Nan didn't even look up.
Unhappily, Tamzin retreated to the hall, took
her coat from the peg and went quietly out
of the house.

chapter three

From the garden gate a path led down the valley towards the beach. Tamzin tramped along, watching the cliffs rising higher to either side. She smelled the sea before she saw it; a sharp, fresh, tangy smell that tingled in her nostrils and helped to clear her head. Then, a little way on, the valley suddenly opened out and there in front of her was the beach.

The tide was low and a huge, deserted expanse of smooth, pale sand stretched away in a great sweep to two massive and craggy headlands. Way out past the headlands were

the white lines of the surf. Tamzin could hear
it roaring, and even from this distance she
could feel the strong wind blowing fine spray
in her face. It was an awe-inspiring scene and
it unnerved her just a little. But she ignored the
feeling and walked down the slope of rocks
and pebbles to the sand.

Beyond the headlands the beach stretched
away and away in both directions. There
were caves and rocks and pools at the foot
of the cliffs, and off to the right a ruined
stone building with a tall chimney teetered
on the clifftop. The ruin looked brooding
and unfriendly so Tamzin turned left and
walked slowly along near the tideline, scuffing
her feet in the sand. She was still badly
shaken by what had happened, and Nan's
fury made her feel even worse. Why hadn't
she listened to Nan's warning? It was as if
someone – or something – else had got into
her mind and made her disobey. Then when
she held the statue, it had seemed to move

by itself. As if it had *wanted* her to break it.

She shivered and stopped walking, turning to gaze out at the sea. It looked grey and cold, and the waves rolled in ferociously, tumbling and clashing against each other. A long way out, a huge rock crag jutted up from the water. Its shape was vague in the low cloud and spray, but she could see white-topped breakers surging around it. It looked menacing and dangerous, and Tamzin turned away, shoving her cold hands into her jeans pockets.

Her fingers felt a small, hard object in one of the pockets. Puzzled, she pulled it out and stared at it. At first she couldn't work out what it could be; it simply looked like a piece of stone with rough edges. But then she turned it over and saw the glittering red chip set into the grey. It was a piece of the broken statue; part of the horse's head. She must have found it during the hunt for the last fragments, put it into her pocket, then forgotten all about it.

* * *

The last thing Tamzin wanted was a
reminder of the statue, and for a moment she
was tempted to fling the piece of stone into the
sea. But then she remembered what Nan had
said about finding all the pieces. Maybe she
wanted to try to mend the statue? Tamzin
thought that she ought to take it back before
Nan discovered it was missing.

She slipped the fragment into her pocket
again and turned to walk back the way she
had come. As she rounded the headland
she saw that she was no longer alone on the
beach. Four ponies were coming towards her.
One was being ridden, while the other three
followed behind on leading reins. Nan had
said there was a riding stable in the valley.
The ponies must have come from there, and
Tamzin watched with quickening interest as
they came towards her. The rider was a dark-
haired boy of about her own age. As they
drew level he saw her staring and pulled his
mount to a halt.

'Hi,' he said.

'Hello.' Tamzin pushed windblown hair out of her face and smiled uncertainly. Then she nodded at the ponies. 'Are they all yours?'

'Yes. Well, my mum and dad's, anyway. Like horses, do you?'

'Oh, yes!' Tamzin thought of the statue and added wryly, 'Real ones, anyway.'

'Do you ride?'

She shook her head. 'I've never learned. But I'd love to.'

The boy grinned. 'Then you've come to the right place! We own the stables up the valley. Are you here on holiday?'

Tamzin shook her head. 'I've come to live with my nan while my parents are in Canada,' she told him. 'Her house is in the valley too. It's called Chapel Cottage.'

'Oh! Then your nan must be Mrs Weston, the artist.' The boy looked surprised. 'We're neighbours, then.' He jumped down from his saddle with an ease that Tamzin wistfully envied. 'My name's Joel Richards. What's yours?'

'Tamzin Weston.' One of the ponies, which was almost pure white with just a hint of dapple grey, pushed its muzzle towards her, and she reached out and stroked it. The pony whickered; she felt his breath on her hand, and his warm, friendly, animal smell tickled her nostrils.

'He's lovely,' she said. 'What's he called?'

'Moonlight,' Joel told her. He pointed to the others one by one. 'And that's Pippin, that's Jester, and the one I'm riding is Sally-Ann.' Moonlight was nuzzling Tamzin's coat now, hoping for titbits. 'He's a greedyguts too!' Joel added. Then: 'What did you mean about only liking *real* horses? Your nan paints them, doesn't she? Don't you like her pictures?'

'Oh, they're brilliant! It isn't that, it's . . .' Tamzin stopped as she realized that she had been just about to blurt out the tale of the grey stone statue to a complete stranger. She shrugged. 'It's a long story.'

'I've got plenty of time.' He saw her doubtful expression. ' No, really. You look as if you want to talk about it. So tell me.'

To her own surprise, and almost before she realized what she was doing, Tamzin did tell him. Joel listened as she described how she had broken the statue, and how Nan had reacted. As she finished she pulled out the fragment she had found in her pocket, saying, 'I'm supposed to have picked up every piece. So I'll have to take this back to Nan before she finds out it's missing, or I'll be in trouble all over again.'

She held the fragment out to show him. Moonlight had been standing quietly, half dozing in the way that horses do, but as Tamzin's hand passed close to his nose, his head suddenly jerked up. His ears went back, his nostrils flared and he shied away with a squealing noise that sounded partly like fear and partly like anger.

'Moonlight!' Hastily Joel grabbed at the reins as it seemed Moonlight might break free and bolt away. 'Steady, boy, steady! What's the matter?'

Tamzin stared at the pony, then at the piece of the broken statue. 'It was this,' she said in a small voice. 'He saw it, and he didn't like it.'

'Oh, come on!' Joel had calmed Moonlight down and was stroking his nose. 'It's only a bit of stone. Here, give it to me.' He took it and held it out towards Moonlight. 'There you are, boy. That's all it is, look.'

Moonlight did look, and with a shudder he backed away, snorting.

Joel was astonished. 'You're right; he doesn't like it. All right, Moonlight, all right.' He shoved the fragment at Tamzin. 'You'd better put it away where he can't see it again.'

An unpleasant thought came to Tamzin. Animals had a sort of sixth sense, didn't they?

* * *

They knew when something was not good to have around. Suddenly she had a powerful urge to be rid of the fragment, not to have it near her any more.

She heard her own voice say, 'I'd rather *throw* it away.'

Joel shrugged. 'Well, throw it away, then.'

'But Nan . . .'

'She won't know if you don't tell her.'

That was true. Tamzin tried to convince herself that she was being silly, that a mere piece of stone couldn't possibly do her any harm. But there had to be a reason for the way Moonlight had behaved when he saw it. And she remembered how, in the moment before she dropped it, the little horse statue had squirmed in her hand.

I don't want anything to do with this! The thought rushed into her mind, and she turned away from Joel and ran towards the sea. She reached the water's edge and stopped. The sound of the breakers seemed to swell and

* ⋆ ⋆ ⋆

roar in her ears, and in the gloom the distant
rock crag loomed like a threat.

Tamzin drew her arm back and hurled the
piece of the statue as far out into the sea as she
could.

She walked back to where Joel waited with
the ponies. 'Better?' he asked.

Tamzin nodded. She *did* feel relieved now
that the fragment was gone. 'I'd better go
back to Nan's,' she said. 'She'll be wondering
where I am.'

'Come up to the stables if you'd like to,' Joel
invited. 'Any time.'

'Thanks. I'd like that.'

He mounted Sally-Ann again, and Tamzin
watched as he and all the ponies trotted away
across the beach for their exercise. The sky
was darkening ominously and in the distance
veils of rain were sweeping across the sea.
Tamzin shivered and hurried back towards the
path. Once, she looked back. Joel and the
ponies were some way off now, but she could

35

* * *

see Moonlight more clearly than the rest. In the ominous light, his white coat seemed to be tinged with blue.

Just like all the horses in Nan's pictures.

chapter four

The wind was rising and Tamzin could feel rain in the air by the time she got back to Chapel Cottage. At first she thought Nan wasn't in. But then she heard noises from the studio. Nan was there, still searching on the floor, and when she heard Tamzin's footsteps she looked up.

'There's a piece of the statue missing!' she said agitatedly. 'I can't find it anywhere!'

Tamzin felt a terrible sense of guilt, and her face reddened. But she couldn't pretend, so she told Nan what she had done.

'I'm sorry, Nan,' she finished. 'I just had to

get rid of it. I couldn't bear having it around me.'

She expected Nan to be furious – but Nan wasn't. Instead she sighed heavily. 'Oh, Tamzin. I can't blame you for feeling that.' She got to her feet, her eyes sad and, Tamzin thought uneasily, just a little frightened. 'What's done is done, and there's no changing it,' she added. 'The statue can't be mended now. I think the best thing I can do is bury it in the garden.'

'Bury it?' Tamzin echoed. 'Why, Nan?'

Nan only shook her head. 'Never mind. We won't talk about it any more. It's better that way.'

'But –'

'*Tamzin.*' Nan's voice became stern. 'I said we won't talk about it.'

She picked up the bag of pieces and went into the kitchen. Tamzin followed, in time to see her opening the back door.

'Can I help?' she asked timidly.

38

'No,' said Nan. She picked up a trowel from the windowsill and took it and the bag outside. From the doorway Tamzin watched as Nan walked to the furthest flowerbed, crouched down and began to dig a hole. It seemed to take her a long time; she dug very deeply, and Tamzin wondered why she should take so much trouble. At last, though, Nan was satisfied. She dropped the bag into the hole and started to fill it in. As she worked, her lips moved. She was muttering something but Tamzin was too far away to hear what it was. She shuffled her feet on the doorstep, feeling uneasy. What was Nan doing? Why had she insisted that the statue must be buried? What was going on?

Nan shovelled the last trowelful of earth into the hole and patted it down. As she started to get up, from the direction of the sea came a sudden deep roar. It sounded like an express train approaching. Tamzin turned towards it, frowning . . .

* * *

An enormous blast of wind came screaming
up the valley and across the garden. It hit
Nan full on and almost bowled her over.
Staggering, she tried to regain her balance, and
Tamzin screamed out to her in terror.

'Nan! *Nan!*'

Her cry was torn from her and flung away,
and she clung desperately to the door frame as
the great wind tried to snatch her off her feet.
Through the tangle of hair that whipped
stingingly across her face she glimpsed Nan
struggling towards the house. Nan's arm
flailed towards Tamzin, and Tamzin reached
out. Their fingers touched, they grasped each
other, and Tamzin pulled with all her strength.

As Nan stumbled over the threshold the
wind vanished. One instant it was howling
over them; the next, they were gasping in
complete stillness and eerie silence. Tamzin
shook her head dizzily; then Nan's voice
broke through her confusion.

'Close the door! And lock it.' Nan went

quickly to the window and jerked it shut. 'We must close them all. Windows, doors, everything!'

Tamzin's voice trembled. 'Wh-why, Nan? What's happening? That wind –'

'It's nothing to be frightened of,' said Nan. 'But there's a storm coming and it's going to be a bad one. It's safer to lock up the house.'

Tamzin knew she wasn't telling the whole truth. There was something else going on; something that Nan didn't want to tell her. *That statue.*

'Nan!' Tamzin began pleadingly. 'What does it *mean*?'

But Nan hurried out of the kitchen, and pretended she hadn't heard.

By late afternoon the wind had risen to a full gale. The clouds darkened until the whole sky was a bruised, angry purplish-black, and soon afterwards the rain came driving in from the sea. Rain squalls hurled themselves up the

valley, as if someone had turned on a gigantic
fire-hose. The outside world was blotted out
by a wall of water, and the whole house shook
and rattled to the stormy wind's rampaging.

Tamzin went to her room straight after
dinner. She switched on the lights, closed the
curtains against the wild evening, and tried
to read a book. But she couldn't concentrate.
The noise of the storm was far louder upstairs
and the lights kept dipping, as if they would
go out at any moment. Tamzin could have
gone down to the warmth and cosiness of the
sitting room but Nan was there, and she felt
a strong urge to stay out of Nan's way.

She was jumpy and unhappy. Dad had
phoned earlier, to say he was home safely,
and she had talked to him and to Mum. She
had wanted to tell them about the statue. But
what was there to tell? She had disobeyed
Nan, Nan had been cross with her, and she
was frightened of a piece of stone? It would
sound silly, so she had said nothing. Anyway,

* * *

if she had blurted the story out Mum and Dad
would have started worrying, and there was
nothing they could actually do. It wouldn't
have been fair to trouble them.

Tamzin picked up her book again, trying
not to listen to the noises of the storm. But it
was impossible to ignore them. Eerily, the
sounds made her think of horses. The
screaming wind was like wild neighing and
the rain hammering on the roof tiles seemed
to echo the sound of drumming, galloping
hooves. *Go away, go away!* Tamzin said
silently and fiercely. *I don't want to listen!
Oh, go aw*–

She yelped, and jumped like a startled rabbit
as suddenly the lights went out. Darkness
engulfed the room. In panic Tamzin fumbled
for the bedside lamp but when she worked the
switch nothing happened.

Fear set her heart thumping as she
scrambled to her feet and tried to find the
door. She bumped into a chair and knocked it

43

over with a crash. At last her hand closed round the doorknob. The landing was dark too. She started to grope her way along, then to her enormous relief a light flickered on the stairs and Nan's voice called from below. 'Tamzin? Are you all right?'

Nan was at the foot of the stairs, a torch in her hand. 'It's a power cut,' she said. 'The wind must have damaged the electricity lines. It often happens in gales and storms. You'd better come down.'

Nan's company was better than the thought of staying alone upstairs in the dark. With the torch beam to help her, Tamzin hastened down the staircase and into the sitting room. There was a fire there, and Nan lit candles in two sconces that stood on the mantelpiece.

'That's better,' she said as the candle flames danced and brightened.

Tamzin looked around. The firelight was welcoming, but beyond it the shadows seemed to crowd in.

* * *

'How long will the power cut last, do you think?' she asked. Her voice was shaky.

'Oh, it probably won't come back on till tomorrow,' Nan told her. She smiled. 'Don't worry, you'll get used to it. And at least the cooker's gas, so we can still make hot drinks!'

She was trying to cheer Tamzin along, and Tamzin suspected she was trying to cheer herself too. That made her feel even more uneasy, and she sat down in a chair close to the fire, suppressing a shiver.

'Would you like to play a game?' Nan asked. 'I've got Scrabble and Monopoly. Or perhaps cards are easier in this light.'

It was better than nothing, so they played Rummy and Chase the Ace for an hour. Then Nan taught Tamzin Clock Patience and left her to it while she went to make some hot chocolate. But Tamzin didn't play Patience. Instead, she sat listening to the storm sounds outside; the ramp and shriek of the wind, the rush and hiss of the rain. It *was* like horses:

mad, wild, dangerous horses, stampeding out of control. Like the cruel little stone horse now buried in pieces in the garden . . .

Suddenly she couldn't bear the tension inside her any more. She jumped up from her chair and ran to the kitchen.

'Nan!' She faced Nan where she stood by the cooker, in the dim light of more candles. 'Nan, I'm frightened! I know there's something going on, and it's all to do with the statue I broke!'

'Tamzin –' Nan began.

'Please, Nan!' Tamzin cried. 'Don't pretend! You see, I saw the words carved on the statue. What do they mean? Are they a curse?' Tears spilled suddenly down her cheeks. 'Oh, Nan, what have I *done*?'

For a moment Nan's face tightened angrily . . . then abruptly the anger collapsed. Putting a hand to her own face, she said, 'Very well. I'll tell you. I didn't want to, but I suppose you've got a right to know.' She drew a deep breath. 'I'll finish making these hot drinks, then we'll go back to the sitting room and talk.'

Outside, the wind screamed an echo that made Tamzin shudder.

chapter five

'It's a very old tale,' said Nan quietly. 'My grandmother told it to me when I was young, and she learned it from her grand-mother long before that.'

They were sitting together on the sofa. Their mugs of chocolate stood on a low table nearby, but neither of them had had so much as a sip yet. Wind rocked the house; rain battered the windows. On the sofa arm, Baggins lay asleep. Tamzin listened as Nan continued.

'That statue has been in our family for hundreds of years,' Nan said. 'The words you

saw carved on the base are in the ancient
Cornish language and they mean "Guard This
Stone". But they're only the first words of
the rhyme.'

She got up and went over to the
bookshelves, where she took out a large, heavy
book with a black cover.

'This is our family Bible,' she said as she
laid it on the table. 'The whole rhyme is here,
in English. One of our ancestors must have
translated it into English years later, and written
it down.' She turned pages, which rustled with
a strange, secretive sound. 'Here it is.'

Tamzin leaned forward, and read:

Guard this stone that prisons me,
For if it should be cast away,
Then I shall come from surging sea,
And turn your world to stormy grey.

The words sent a chill through her. 'It's a
curse,' she whispered and looked fearfully at
Nan. 'Isn't it?'

Nan sighed. 'I don't know, and that's the truth. No one knows any more. All I can tell you is what my grandmother told me, and that was little enough.'

The flames of the fire dipped and flickered as wind roared in the chimney. The candles guttered and Baggins growled softly in his sleep. 'Go on,' said Tamzin. 'Please, Nan.'

'Well . . . there was an old legend about two spirits that haunted this coast long, long ago. They were known as the Blue Horse and the Grey Horse, and it was said that they came from the sea. The Blue Horse was a benevolent spirit. He brought fair winds and calm water, and protected the sailors and fishermen when they were at sea. But the Grey Horse was cruel. He brought storms and treacherous tides; he hated all humans, and took delight in wrecking ships and drowning the sailors on board.'

Nan paused, gazing into the fire. 'My grandmother was very old when she told me this story, and she couldn't remember all of it. But a time came when the Grey Horse tried to overcome the Blue Horse and destroy him. The two spirits fought a terrible battle. There were storms and gales and huge, raging tides, and the people of the coast were terrified, for it seemed that the Grey Horse would win and destroy them all. But one fisherman's family were determined to help the Blue Horse. I don't know how they did it: the tale is so old that that part of it's long lost. But somehow that family joined forces with the Blue Horse, and between them they overcame the Grey Horse and defeated him.'

Nan turned to the table again. 'When the battle was over and the people were safe, the eldest woman of the fisherman's family – she was very wise and people believed she had second sight – carved a stone statue. The legend says that the evil power of the Grey Horse was imprisoned in the statue, and the family pledged to keep it for always.' She turned a piercing, searching gaze on Tamzin. 'You've guessed who they were, haven't you?' Tamzin's expression gave everything away, and Nan nodded. 'That's right. They were our ancestors. And the legend also says that if the statue should ever be broken, the dark spirit will be released again.'

Silence fell. Even the sounds of the storm seemed to have paused for a few moments, and Tamzin felt a tight, choking sensation in her chest. At last, in a tiny, quavering voice, she whispered, 'And I broke it.'

Nan looked away. 'How were you to know? Maybe I should have told you before. Maybe I should have explained from the start.' She sighed. 'I inherited the statue from my grand-mother. She told me to take great care of it and never let it out of my keeping. It was our duty, she said, to keep faith with the Blue Horse, and keep the Grey Horse's evil power at bay. And in time, I was to pass that duty on

⋆ ⋆ ⋆

to my eldest granddaughter, as our ancestors have done for centuries.'

'Your eldest granddaughter is me . . .' Tamzin whispered.

'Yes. You're so young, though. I didn't want to tell you until you were older. I hoped you wouldn't visit me, so you wouldn't see the statue. But then your parents had to go to Canada, and there was no one else to look after you.'

Tamzin stared at the rhyme in the old Bible again. *Guard this stone that prisons me, For if it should be cast away* . . . The meaning was all too clear, and she began to shiver.

Nan took hold of her hand. 'Don't be frightened, Tamzin. It's only a tale. In the old days people used to believe all kinds of foolish things, but we're more sensible now, aren't we? Maybe it isn't true. Maybe there's no such thing as the Grey Horse.'

'But if there is,' said Tamzin, 'what will it do? What *can* it do?'

53

*   *   *

Nan sighed. 'I don't know, love. We'll just have to wait and see.'

Tamzin desperately wanted to believe that the Grey Horse was just a legend. But she had felt the angry power in the statue. If that power had now been set free, what would it mean for her and Nan?

'Nan,' she asked, 'what happened to the Blue Horse after the battle was over?'

'The legend doesn't say,' Nan replied. 'He seems simply to have vanished.' She smiled an odd little smile. 'I know what you're thinking. Years ago I started painting blue horses because I hoped they might somehow call up the good spirit, to help me guard the statue. But I don't think they ever did. Even if the Blue Horse exists, no one knows how to reach him any more.'

They both fell silent. Tamzin looked at her still untouched mug, but she felt too queasy to drink. A sense of dread had lodged inside her like a tight, hard knot, and she was very

* * *

frightened. Then Nan took her hand again.

'It's getting late,' she said. 'You'd better go to bed now.' Her fingers squeezed Tamzin's kindly. 'Try not to think about the Grey Horse, mmm? The storm will be gone by morning, and all these dark things will seem much brighter.'

Tamzin didn't argue. Upstairs, with a reassuring nightlight, she snuggled deep under her duvet and tried to do as Nan had said. But how could she not think about the Grey Horse? A spirit of storms and treacherous tides, Nan had called it. Was tonight's storm an omen? Did it mean that the Grey Horse was coming back to wreak havoc, as the old rhyme warned?

And if the Grey Horse was coming back, what could anyone do to stop it?

Suddenly, mingling with the noises of the wind and rain outside, Tamzin heard something new. She tensed, listening, and after a few moments she heard it again.

It sounded like distant whinnying.

She sat bolt upright. It was the storm, it must be. All evening the screaming of the wind had been making her think of horses. There couldn't possibly be a real horse out there.

The sound came a third time, and she jumped violently. It *was* a horse's neigh – and now it was right outside in the garden.

Tamzin scrambled out of bed and rushed to the window. She didn't even think about being frightened; she had to know what was out there. Pulling back the curtain, she peered out into the wild night. For a few seconds she couldn't see anything. Then, as her eyes adjusted to the darkness, she glimpsed a large, dark shape moving among the bushes.

It was a horse. There could be no doubt of it. Tamzin saw its mane tossing in the wind, the smooth, sleek shape of its neck, the gleam of its eyes. Fear hit her. She drew a huge

breath to scream for Nan – and the dark
shape wasn't there any more.

Shocked, Tamzin stood staring at the
place where the horse had been. It hadn't
galloped away. It *couldn't* have done in such
a short time. It had simply vanished into
thin air.

Slowly she let the curtain drop. Her heart
was thumping and she didn't know what to
think. Had the horse really been there? She
was so wound up that she could easily have
imagined the whole thing. Or maybe she'd
been half asleep, and the sound and the dark
shape had been a sort of waking dream.

With a shiver she turned back to her bed.
As she did so, Nan's painting caught her eye.
The blue horse, galloping out of a sea under
a full moon . . . In the dim, flickering glow of
the nightlight the picture looked so real and
alive. And as Tamzin looked at it, it seemed to
her that it really did come to life. She saw the
waves surging, saw the horse racing towards

her, as if it would burst out of the picture
frame and into the room.

The illusion only lasted for a moment,
then it was gone and the painting was still
again. Tamzin stared. She should have been
frightened but she wasn't. Instead, she felt
a strange sense of peace washing over her; the
complete opposite of the feeling she had had
from the Grey Horse's statue. It was silly,
it was crazy, but she could almost believe that
the horse in the painting had been galloping
towards her to protect her.

Without knowing why, she whispered, '*Blue
Horse . . . ?*' There was no answer, of course.
The horse in the painting did not move again.
But Tamzin felt comforted.

She went back to bed, and lay gazing
steadily at the picture until she fell asleep.

chapter six

By morning the storm was gone. The wind was still blustery and flurries of rain blew up the valley, but by the time Tamzin and Nan sat down to breakfast the sun was breaking through.

The electricity had come on again and Nan chatted cheerfully about everyday things, almost as if their talk last night had never happened. But it had happened and Tamzin couldn't forget. Nor could she forget the dark shape she had glimpsed in the garden. However, a thought had occurred to her. Hadn't Joel said that the riding stable where he lived was just a short way up the valley? One of the horses could have got out during the night and strayed along the valley path to Chapel Cottage. It was a rational explanation and she very much wanted to believe it.

Desperate to be sure, Tamzin said, 'Nan, is it all right if I go to the riding stable this morning?'

Nan looked up from her toast. 'The riding stable? Oh, of course, you met Joel yesterday, didn't you?' She smiled. 'Yes, if you've been invited, you can go. Who knows: if you make yourself useful, you might be able to earn some riding lessons!'

So a short while later, Tamzin set off. As she headed for the gate that led to the valley path, she looked carefully at the garden. There was no sign of any trampling, which was strange. But then perhaps she had scared the straying horse off before it could do any damage.

The path ran between the high cliff

headlands. It was a wet, muddy, uphill walk, and by the time the stables came in sight Tamzin's legs were aching. A big wooden gate led to the stable yard and as she approached it Tamzin saw Joel sweeping out an empty stall. She called his name and he looked up.

'Hi!' He came to meet her, but Tamzin was anxiously scanning the row of stables with ponies' heads looking out of the open top doors.

'The horses,' she said as Joel reached her. 'Are they all here?'

Joel looked baffled. 'Of course. Shouldn't they be?' He saw her expression and frowned. 'What's the matter?'

She told him what had happened during the night. 'I thought it was one of your horses,' she finished. 'I thought maybe it had got out and . . .' Her voice tailed off. Her heart was bumping and she didn't like the feeling.

Joel shook his head. 'No, it wasn't one of ours. Couldn't have been.'

* ★ ★

Tamzin swallowed. 'Has anyone else round here got horses?'

'Not close enough for one to have found its way down the valley. Tamzin, what's up? You look scared.'

She wanted to tell him that she was scared, and why. But if she did, she would have to explain about the Grey Horse. How could she expect Joel to believe her? He would say it was just a silly story. He would probably laugh and tease her, and that would make things worse than ever. So with a great effort she forced herself to smile and tried to sound casual as she said, 'Oh, I was just a bit worried, that's all. I mean, if the horse had escaped, and it hurt itself . . .'

'Horses aren't daft,' Joel reassured her. 'Anyway, it might have been something else – or nothing at all. It sounds to me as if you dreamed it.'

'Yes,' said Tamzin. 'Maybe I did.' And she thought, *I wish I could believe that.*

* * *

Joel said, 'Well, now you're here, how about helping me with the mucking out?' He grinned. 'Then if Mum says it's OK, I'll give you your first riding lesson. You said you want to learn, didn't you?'

Tamzin's worries about the Grey Horse melted away and her face lit up. 'Oh, yes!' she said. 'I'd love to!'

Mucking out was hard, smelly work but Tamzin didn't mind in the least. For the first time in her life she was involved with horses, and she loved it. She forked soiled straw out of the stalls, put down fresh, then helped Joel to fill all the water buckets from the tap in the yard. She made friends with more of the ponies, and also with three cats and a big dog called Barney, who looked like a woolly hay-stack and slobbered happily all over her jeans. She was delighted when Moonlight seemed to recognize her, and spent a long time stroking his muzzle and talking to him.

* * *

'He really likes you,' Joel said, coming into
Moonlight's stall with a net full of fresh,
sweet hay. 'You can ride him on your lesson.
He's ideal for a beginner.' He hung up the hay
net. 'There! That's everything done. Come on
then, we'll take the ponies to the yard and
saddle up.'

They were in time to wave goodbye to
Joel's mother, Mrs Richards, who was taking
two late-season holiday couples out for an
hour's ride. Tamzin was glad Mrs Richards
wasn't there to see her first efforts with
Moonlight's harness. Putting the saddle on
was easy enough, but the bridle was much
more difficult. It seemed to be an endless
tangle of straps and buckles, and Tamzin
muddled the whole thing three times before
Joel came to her rescue.

'Never mind,' he said. 'The more you do it,
the easier it'll get.' He slipped the snaffle bit
into Moonlight's mouth, pulled the bridle over
the pony's head and buckled the strap called

the throatlash. 'Right. Just a hard hat, and
we're ready.'

With a borrowed riding helmet firmly on,
Tamzin really felt 'the biz', as Joel put it. He
showed her how to mount, gathering the reins
and placing her hands on Moonlight's back,
then putting her left foot in the stirrup.

'One, two, three and *up*!' He gave her a
helping shove and suddenly Tamzin was
sitting in the saddle, with the ground a lot
further away than it had been a moment ago.

'Wow!' she said, feeling that if she smiled
any more widely her face would fall in half.
'This is great!' She had forgotten all her earlier
worries; forgotten everything but the fact that
her dearest wish had come true. Joel clipped a
leading rein to Moonlight's bridle, then sprang
with an ease that Tamzin envied on to the
back of a piebald pony called Dandy.

'All right?' he asked.

Tamzin nodded eagerly.

'Good. Then hold the reins like I showed

you, press your heels gently against his flanks, and we're off.'

With Dandy ahead and Moonlight on the leading rein, they rode slowly out of the yard. Tamzin's heart thudded with excitement and pride, and she tried to remember the instructions Joel had given her. Back straight, knees in, heels down. Reins not too tight but not too loose, so that she could just 'feel' Moonlight's mouth. As they turned on to the valley path she swayed to the swing of the pony's stride, gazing around and feeling – almost literally – on top of the world.

Joel looked over his shoulder and nodded encouragement. 'That's it! You're doing fine.'

Halfway to the beach they met some walkers coming the other way. Joel edged Dandy into the heather to let them pass; Moonlight followed and Tamzin smiled at the walkers, trying to look as if she had ridden horses all her life. When they moved on again she dared to take one hand off the reins and pat Moonlight's neck where his thick white mane curved over. Moonlight's ears pricked and he made a small whickering sound, as if he was pleased.

Soon they were in sight of the beach. The tide was low again. Two people and a dog were walking in the distance, but there was no one else in sight.

'Would you like to ride on the sand?' Joel asked.

'Well, if you think I can.' Tamzin gazed at the beach stretching away into the distance. 'But we're not going to gallop or anything, are we?'

He laughed. 'Course not! It's much too soon for you. Though we might try a little trot, if you want to.'

The ponies picked their way down the rocks, and Joel taught Tamzin how to lean back in the saddle, to make the slope easier for Moonlight. The wind was stronger on the beach and the sea was very rough after the storm, surf pounding in with a huge, steady noise that beat against Tamzin's ears and seemed to echo inside her head.

'The lion's roaring today,' said Joel.

She was puzzled. 'What do you mean?'

He pointed to where the huge crag rose from the sea in the distance. 'See that? People round here call it Lion Rock, so when the sea's really big like this, they say it's the lion roaring.'

For some reason that she couldn't work out, a peculiar feeling fluttered in Tamzin's stomach. 'It's a weird name,' she said. 'Why do they call it that?'

Joel shrugged. 'I don't know. Maybe they think it looks like a lion's head or something, though I can't see how. Anyway, how about trying that trot? Shorten your reins a little bit, press with your heels, and try to rise up and down with the trotting rhythm. Ready? Right. Let's go!'

Rising to the trot was tricky, but Tamzin

began to get the hang of it as Joel led her
along the beach. They weren't going very fast,
but it was still exhilarating, with the wind
blowing in her face and the quick thudding of
the ponies' hooves mingling with the sea's
thunder.

And then the disaster happened.

From the corner of her eye Tamzin had seen
the big wave rising out to sea. But she didn't
realize just how big it was until it raced in
close to the shore and started to curl over. Its
crest seemed to form the shape of a horse's
head . . . then it broke with a tremendous
crash. Moonlight uttered a shrill neigh and
reared. Tamzin slid backwards as he raked the
air, only to be thrown forward again as his
front hooves came down with a bone-shaking
thump. The leading rein was snatched from
Joel's hand and Moonlight bolted, careering
away along the beach with Tamzin clinging to
his back and screaming in terror.

chapter seven

'**M**oonlight, stop! Oh, help! *Stop!*'

But there was nothing Tamzin could do to stop the pony's wild gallop. She clung on desperately. Joel on Dandy was chasing her, but Moonlight was faster. They raced along the tideline and to her horror Tamzin saw that the huge wave was racing with them, running at an angle to all the others. It still had the shape of a horse's head. And its tumbling foam wasn't white, but *grey*.

Then out to sea another, much bluer wave rose. Through her flying hair Tamzin glimpsed it speeding towards the shore, on a collision course with the horse-shaped breaker. The two waves met in a shuddering clash, and spray fountained skywards. Moonlight swerved from the water, reared again, and Tamzin lost her grip and pitched out of the saddle.

She hit the ground with a force that knocked all the air out of her lungs, and lay winded on the sand. Moonlight came to a snorting halt. He swung to face the sea, and stamped and pawed at the waves as if he was challenging them. Then as Tamzin giddily started to sit up, he turned towards her and put his muzzle down to her face as if to say he was sorry.

Dandy came galloping up and Joel sprang off his back. 'Tamzin! Are you all right?'

'I . . . think so,' said Tamzin shakily. She let Joel help her to her feet, then he rounded on Moonlight.

'You stupid animal! What got into you?'

'Don't be angry with him!' Tamzin pleaded. She was shocked and would have a few bruises, but there was no real damage. 'It was that big wave. It frightened him . . .' Her voice tailed off. Moonlight was staring out to sea again. He was making strange, angry whickering sounds, and his attention seemed to be fixed on the distant, hazy shape of Lion Rock.

'What's he looking at now?' said Joel. 'Moonlight! Calm down, there's nothing out there!'

A chill went through Tamzin and she thought, *Isn't there?* Moonlight was between her and the sea, and she had a feeling that he was trying to shield her from it. She thought of the wave, with its grey crest like a horse's head. And the second wave, dazzlingly blue, that had rushed in to meet and clash with it. Then she remembered the first time she had met Joel on the beach. Moonlight had been with him, and against the background of the gathering storm, the pony's coat had taken on a peculiar blue tinge.

She said in a small voice, 'It wasn't just the wave that scared him.'

'What do you mean?' Joel was baffled.

'I mean . . . there was something else.'

'Like what?'

'I don't know. But it wasn't an ordinary wave. Didn't you see it? Its top was shaped like a horse's head. And when it broke, its crest wasn't white, it was grey!'

'I don't understand. A wave's just a wave; it –'

'But it *wasn't* just a wave!' Suddenly Tamzin felt frightened, and almost before she knew it she was telling Joel everything that had happened last night. Nan's story, the rhyme in the old Bible, how the shape in the garden suddenly vanished – and the eerie moment when Nan's painting had seemed to come to life.

'It made me think of Moonlight,' she said. 'When I first met you on the beach, his coat looked blue against the storm clouds, just like

the horse in the picture. Last night I . . . I
thought it was protecting me. And now . . .
I've got this weird feeling that Moonlight
wants to protect me, too. That's why he bolted
when that wave broke. He was trying to get
me away from it.'

'So you think it had something to do with
this Grey Horse?'

Tamzin bit her lip, hesitated, then nodded.
'Yes.'

'Oh, come on, Tam! Magic horses, evil
spirits – it's all a bit far-fetched!' Joel peered
more closely at her. 'Are you sure you didn't
bump your head when you fell?'

'I didn't! You saw the wave!'

'I wasn't looking at any waves. I was trying
to catch Moonlight.'

Her face fell. 'So you don't believe me.'

'Well . . .' Joel sighed. 'I'm not saying there
isn't a legend, like your nan told you. But you
don't honestly think it's true, do you?'

'I don't know!' Tamzin said in distress. 'But

★ ★ ★

weird things have been happening ever since I broke that statue. The storm, and the horse in the garden; and now the wave and Moonlight bolting.'

'Moonlight's just an ordinary pony,' Joel insisted. 'He was scared by a big breaker. That's all there is to it. As for all the other things, it's coincidence, Tam. It can't possibly be anything else.'

She wasn't going to convince him, Tamzin could see. 'OK,' she said dismally. 'I expect you're right, and I'm being an idiot. But will you do something for me?'

'It depends,' said Joel cautiously. 'What is it?'

'Help me look for that missing piece of the statue that I threw into the sea yesterday.'

He stared at her. 'You're joking! It could be anywhere.'

'Maybe. But I've got a feeling we might find it.'

'One little bit of stone, among thousands on

this beach?' Joel made a snorting noise, like a horse. 'Some chance!'

'I'm going to try,' Tamzin persisted doggedly. 'And if I do find it, it'll make me feel a lot better.' She frowned at him. 'Will you help me or not?'

There was a pause, then Joel sighed. 'OK,' he said. 'I'll help. But I still think it's a crazy idea.'

Tamzin didn't answer that, but turned at once towards the tumbled rocks at the foot of the cliffs. Joel followed, leading the ponies. Moonlight was subdued now and walked quietly, though now and again he looked back at the sea.

They started to search. They combed shallow pools, dug among piles of seaweed, sifted sand and stones. Tamzin worked with all her concentration, until at last she was forced to stop for a minute to ease her back, which ached from bending. Joel was a little way off, with the ponies. He had given up

searching, and Tamzin was beginning to
understand why. The piece of the statue could
be anywhere among the rocks and pools and
seaweed. The sea might have carried it away.
Or it might be lying at the bottom of a deep
pool, far out of reach. But Tamzin didn't want
to give up. She hadn't looked in any of the
caves yet. There was a large one nearby and
she went towards it. It was dank and gloomy
and as she ventured in she could hear water
dripping. It was a dismal echoey sound, and
when she called out, 'Come on!' to Joel, her
voice echoed too.

Joel appeared at the cave mouth. 'Tam,
there's no point,' he said. 'It's as dark as a
mine. Even if the piece was in there, you'd
never see it.'

She sighed. He was right; this was hope-
less. And the cave was giving her the creeps. It
was like being in the mouth of a huge animal,
which might at any moment clamp its jaws
shut.

'Never mind,' Joel said as she trailed disconsolately outside again. 'It wouldn't have made any difference if you'd found it. It's only a story, after all.'

Tamzin said, 'Yes,' because she didn't want to argue, then shivered.

'You're cold,' said Joel, 'and your back's all damp where you fell on the sand. We'd better go back, before you catch a chill.'

She nodded. She did feel cold, and dispirited. Moonlight was subdued, too, and as they mounted and set off, his head hung low as if in defeat.

They rode slowly back along the beach and on to the valley path. Joel tried to cheer Tamzin up by talking. He asked about her family, her home, her school, then said, 'I suppose you'll be going to the local school next week, when half term finishes.'

'Yes, I suppose I will,' Tamzin said reluctantly. The prospect of having to face a new school, new people, new ways of doing

things, had been worrying her anyway, but
after what had happened in the last few
days, she simply hadn't wanted to think
about it at all. 'What's it like?' she asked
uneasily.

'Oh, it's pretty good, as schools go,' Joel
reassured her. 'I won't be there, though. I go
to school in Truro now. You'll probably be
in Mrs Beck's class. You'll like her. She's
interested in legends, too.' He grinned. 'She
might even know about the Grey Horse story
and if she doesn't, you can tell her.'

'No!' said Tamzin, so sharply that
Moonlight tossed his head in surprise.

'Steady, Moonlight!' Joel put out a hand to
the white pony's nose, then looked curiously
at Tamzin. 'OK. Sorry if I said the wrong
thing!'

'No, I'm sorry too,' she said. 'I didn't mean
to snap. It's just that I promised Nan I
wouldn't talk about it. I shouldn't even have
told you.'

'Oh, right. Well, don't worry, I won't say anything to anyone else.'

'Promise?' Tamzin had to be sure.

Joel nodded. 'Promise. If you don't want me to.'

They rode on, trotting again where the path was level and wide enough, and soon Chapel Cottage was in sight. Tamzin dismounted the way Joel had shown her. She still felt shaky as she patted Moonlight's neck.

'Do you want another lesson soon?' Joel asked.

Tamzin nodded, trying to push thoughts of the Grey Horse from her mind. 'Yes, please,' she said. 'Except . . . I ought to pay for them. And I don't suppose I can afford it.'

He smiled. 'What about helping at the stables, in exchange for lessons?'

'Could I? Really?'

'I should think so. I'll ask Mum about it and phone you later.'

'All right.' Tamzin said her goodbyes, then

***

gave Moonlight a final hug. 'See you again
soon, Moonlight,' she whispered. 'And . . .
thank you.'

She was thanking him for more than the
ride, and the pony snuffed her hair softly,
as though he understood. Then he, Joel and
Dandy were gone, trotting on up the valley as
Tamzin turned in at the gate of Chapel
Cottage.

chapter eight

Nan was in the studio. She was sitting at her easel, working on the half-finished sky-and-sea scene that Tamzin had seen before. She said 'Hello,' but vaguely; she was concentrating hard on the picture.

Tamzin moved round until she could see the canvas. It was going to be another horse picture. Nan was sketching in the horse's outline; it stood facing out to sea with its head high and one forehoof raised.

Suddenly Nan gave a sigh and put her brush down.

'It's no good,' she said in a strange, tense

* * *

voice. 'It just won't come right.' She blinked,
and seemed to see Tamzin properly for the
first time. 'Oh! Sorry, Tamzin, love. I was
miles away. Did you have fun at the stable?'

'Yes thanks, Nan.' Tamzin hesitated.
'What's wrong with the picture?'

'It's the horse. I can't get the outline right.
That isn't like me; I usually . . . oh, never
mind. Perhaps I'll try again later. Only . . .'

'Only what?' Tamzin prompted.

Nan paused, then shook her head. 'It
doesn't matter.' Abruptly she gave Tamzin a
bright, artificial smile. 'I expect you're hungry,
aren't you? I'd better think about lunch.'

She got up from the easel and hurried out
of the studio. Tamzin stared after her. Nan
was worried, there was no doubt of that. But
she obviously didn't want to explain, and
Tamzin didn't want to press her. Nor,
suddenly, did she want to tell Nan what had
happened on the beach. What good would it
do? If Nan heard the story, it would only

* * *

worry her more. It was better to say nothing.

She looked again at the picture. The unfinished horse was like a dim ghost, with the sea visible through it. For no sensible reason Tamzin's spine prickled. Then she left the studio, closing the door carefully behind her.

Tamzin's parents rang at tea time, to say goodbye before their flight left for Canada. Nan tactfully went out of the room. When the call was finished and she came back, she was in time to see Tamzin hastily wiping her eyes.

'Are you all right?' Nan asked sympathetically.

Tamzin nodded, though she wasn't really. 'It's just that Canada seems such a long way away. And a whole *year* . . .'

'Well, we'll just have to make sure it's a busy year, so the time passes quickly,' said Nan, then added, 'And a happy one, too, of course.'

84

* * *

Tamzin looked at her. 'Do you think it will be happy?'

'Well, that's up to us, isn't it? I'm sure we can have a lovely time.' Then Nan quickly changed the subject. 'Anyway, how are your mum and dad? All ready, and everything on time?'

Tamzin nodded again. 'Dad's put something in the post,' she said. 'A going-away present, but he wouldn't tell me what it is.'

'Has he? That's something to look forward to, then. Now, what would you like to do after tea? We could play cards again. Or Scrabble, or even chess. Can you play chess?'

'No. I've never tried.'

'Oh, it's a terrific game. I'll teach you, if you like.'

She was trying hard to make Tamzin feel better but Tamzin knew there was more to it than the matter of Mum and Dad. She wanted to ask about the unfinished horse picture, and why Nan had been so worried.

* * *

But Nan's bracing cheerfulness was like a barrier that she couldn't cross. Whatever it was that troubled her, she was determined to forget about it and she wanted Tamzin to forget it, too.

That, though, was going to be hard for Tamzin to do.

Joel rang later that evening. Tamzin was feeling down, but she brightened when she heard what he had to say.

'Mum says it's fine about swapping riding lessons for help at the stable,' he told her. 'So long as your nan agrees.'

'I'm sure she will!' Tamzin felt her spirits lifting. 'When can I come?'

'How about tomorrow? It's Sunday; we get busy on Sundays, so you can make yourself useful.'

'Great!'

'OK. Moonlight'll be pleased, too. Do you know, he's been really restless since we got back? He keeps staring around and whinnying. It's almost as if he's looking for you.'

'Honestly?' Tamzin felt a peculiar little inward lurch.

'Yeah. He's taken to you in a big way. Funny, isn't it, how animals sometimes do that?'

'Yes,' said Tamzin as the little lurch came again. 'It is.'

'Oh, well. See you tomorrow then.'

'Yes,' she said again. 'See you.'

Tamzin couldn't sleep that night. She was thinking about Mum and Dad on their long flight, hoping they were all right and would land safely. But she was also thinking about the Grey Horse.

By midnight Nan still hadn't gone to bed. Tamzin could hear faint noises from the studio. Was Nan working on the horse painting again? Why was it so important that she should get it right? It was as if she believed something awful would happen if she didn't, and that thought made Tamzin shiver.

She could dimly see the painting of the galloping horse on the wall, and she stared hard at it until the shivery feeling went away. The horse looked very much like Moonlight, and she remembered what Joel had said earlier about the pony taking a liking to her. It fitted with her own thoughts; the feeling that Moonlight had protected her on the beach today and her certainty that, somehow, there was a connection between him and the Blue Horse.

On an impulse she switched on the lamp, got out of bed and fetched her notebook and pencil from a drawer. She had been trying to keep a diary this year but kept forgetting, so most of the book was blank. Taking the pencil, Tamzin started to sketch a horse. She didn't think she was much good at drawing but she tried to copy, as best she could remember it, the standing horse in Nan's

* * *

troublesome picture. Strangely, the lines came
easily to her and within minutes she had
finished. On the whole it wasn't too bad.
Encouraged, she turned the page and began on
another. This time, in her mind's eye, it was
Moonlight, trotting. She couldn't get the legs
right, and hooves were very difficult, so in the
end she drew some long grass to cover them.
But it did look a *little* bit like Moonlight.

Tamzin yawned. She had a pack of coloured
pencils; she ought to use them to add some
life to the picture. But she really was tired
now. The sounds from the studio had stopped,
so Nan would probably go to bed soon. She,
too, should try to sleep.

She put the notebook down and switched
her light off. This time she fell asleep, and she
dreamed of horses and the sea and, strangely,
ringing bells.

She slept right through until morning. When
she woke up, the first thing she saw was the
open notebook beside her bed. There was her

drawing of Moonlight – but something was different. She stared, then realized what it was.

The trotting pony in her picture had been coloured in blue.

Tamzin frowned. She had been going to colour the picture last night, but she had only meant to do the sky and the grass. This, though . . . Had Nan tiptoed in while she was asleep and coloured it for her? She was sure Nan wouldn't do that. So had she done it herself but been too sleepy to remember? It was the only likely explanation, wasn't it?

She didn't know the answer to the question, and wasn't sure that she wanted to. Carefully she closed the notebook and put it back in the drawer. Then she started to get ready for breakfast.

Sunday was a memorable and exciting day. Tamzin arrived at the stables early, to find Joel and his parents mucking out the ponies' stalls. Mrs Richards welcomed Tamzin like an old friend. Mr Richards, whom she hadn't met before, was big and jovial with a booming voice; he told awful jokes that made her laugh. Barney, the hairy dog, followed her around, slobbering happily, and by the time the mucking out was finished Tamzin felt almost like one of the family.

The stable had lots of Sunday bookings and they were kept busy all morning, grooming and saddling ponies and helping the people who came for their rides. Tamzin felt a funny little pang as she saw Moonlight trot out of the yard with a small boy on his back, but she pushed the feeling away and threw herself into the work.

She was invited to lunch, and when they had finished and she couldn't manage another mouthful, Joel said, 'Moonlight and Sally-Ann aren't booked this afternoon, Dad. Can I give Tamzin another lesson?'

'Good idea,' said Mr Richards. 'Don't go on the beach, though; the tide will be coming in.

Why not ride to the village?' He smiled at
Tamzin. 'It's good practice, and I don't
suppose you've had much chance to see it yet.'

'I haven't seen it at all,' Tamzin admitted.
'But am I good enough yet, with traffic and
everything?'

Mrs Richards laughed. 'Don't worry, it's
not like the city! Anyway, Joel will look after
you. And you can get me some shopping at the
minimart. I'll give you a list.'

After what had happened yesterday, Tamzin
was privately relieved that they wouldn't be
going to the beach again. She made a better
job of putting Moonlight's bridle on, and
soon she and Joel were setting off.

The village was a mile away, and was bigger
than she remembered from when she had
driven through it with Dad. As well as the
mini-supermarket there was a butcher, a
baker, a greengrocer, a newsagent, a little post
office and a gallery selling paintings and
pottery and gifts.

* * *

They rode sedately along the main street.
People smiled and waved – Joel seemed to
know nearly everyone – and the smiles were so
friendly that by the time they reached the end
of the village Tamzin's spirits were lifting. The
supermarket was open, so they dismounted
and Joel let Tamzin hold the ponies while he
went in for his mother's shopping. The afternoon was pleasantly warm, and Tamzin
stroked Moonlight's neck as he and Sally-Ann
stood dozing in the sunshine. She felt better
than she had done since arriving in Cornwall.
Daylight, especially sunny daylight, made
everything look different. So many strange
and frightening things had been happening
to her that it was an enormous relief to be
doing something as ordinary as shopping in
the village, where everything was normal and
there was nothing to be afraid of. She felt
happy. So happy that when Joel came out of
the shop she gave him a huge smile that
surprised him.

'What's that for?' he asked.

'Oh, nothing special,' said Tamzin. 'I was only thinking how nice it is to have made a new friend so quickly.' She looked at Moonlight. '*Two* new friends.'

'Well, that's good.' Joel returned her smile with a grin of his own. 'No more creeps, then? After yesterday?'

'No,' she said firmly. 'None. You're right; it's just a story. Isn't it?'

'Of course it is,' said Joel.

Tamzin turned to Moonlight again and Joel watched as she patted the pony affectionately. There was a strange expression on his face; thoughtful, and a little bit troubled. Tamzin wasn't looking at him and so didn't see.

They remounted their ponies and rode on.

chapter nine

Tamzin's parents phoned on Sunday
evening. It was just a quick call to say
that they had arrived safely in Canada but it
cheered Tamzin enormously, and she slept
soundly that night.

The next morning, Monday, she was to start
at the village school, and as she was getting
ready the postman brought her a parcel from
Mum and Dad. Inside was a mobile phone. It
was a trendy one, amazingly small and in the
latest style. And it was blue.

'Now you can show off to all your new
school friends,' Dad said in his letter. 'We've

sent Nan some money for you to buy top-up cards, but don't go TOO crazy with it, will you?'

Tamzin was delighted, and tucked the phone and the letter into her new school bag. She was also secretly pleased by the colour. Even though Dad couldn't have known, she didn't think it was a coincidence. That made her feel good – and she needed to. For the last couple of days, since Moonlight had bolted with her on the beach, nothing strange or frightening had happened. She was relieved; of course she was. But always there, at the back of her mind, was the thought: *How long will this last? What's lying in wait around the next corner?* She was trying hard not to worry about it, but it wasn't easy. Now, though, the present from Mum and Dad was like a signal. Something *blue*. It helped to boost her confidence.

The feeling came back, though, when Nan drove her to school. It was raining hard, pelting grey curtains that the car's windscreen wipers could hardly cope with. Trying to peer through the downpour, Tamzin remembered the storm. Did it *always* rain this much in Cornwall? she asked herself uneasily. Or was this something new, something different? The words of the ancient rhyme in Nan's Bible came sharply back to her. *Then I shall come from surging sea, And turn your world to stormy grey* . . . She wanted to ask Nan about the rain, almost plead with her to say that it wasn't unusual and there was nothing to be afraid of. But Nan was concentrating, and somehow Tamzin didn't have the courage to say what she wanted to.

Groups of children were hurrying out of the rain and into school as Nan stopped the car at the gates. Another pang hit Tamzin. It wasn't the prospect of facing new surroundings. It was the knowledge that for the next few hours she would be away from Nan and from Chapel Cottage, which – despite what had

* * *

happened during the storm – felt like a safe
haven. It was a foolish fear, she told herself,
but it was there all the same.

'All right?' Nan asked, looking at her
searchingly.

Nan understood . . . Tamzin nodded. 'Yes,
thanks, Nan. I'm fine. Really I am.'

'Good,' said Nan. 'Well, you have fun,
now.'

Tamzin smiled and told herself firmly that
there was nothing to be scared of. She kissed
Nan goodbye, took a deep breath and walked
confidently up the drive.

School turned out to be uneventful and
much better than she had expected. There
were only about twenty pupils in her class,
and she was surprised and pleased by how
friendly they all were. Most of them knew
Nan, or at least knew about her, and at break
time they asked Tamzin all about her home,
how it compared to Cornwall, and whether
she had any brothers, sisters or pets. Almost

all the class loved horses, she discovered;
quite a few went riding, and two even had
their own ponies. The class teacher – Mrs
Beck, as Joel had predicted – was young and
blonde and friendly, and the classroom itself
was roomy and airy and painted a cheerful
sunshine yellow, with drawings and charts
and photographs of the local coast and
countryside on the walls.

By the end of the day, when Nan came to
collect her, Tamzin had settled in and had all
but forgotten her other troubles. It had even
stopped raining. She rang Joel that evening,
telling him about her new phone and her
first school day. The evenings were drawing
in fast, so by the time tea was over there
wouldn't be enough daylight left for riding.
But they agreed that Tamzin would be at the
stables first thing on Saturday morning, and
Tamzin went to bed feeling easier than she
had done for days.

The whole week was quiet and uneventful –

* * *

almost *too* uneventful, Tamzin thought sometimes, when she was lying in bed and waiting
for sleep to come. *And turn your world to
stormy grey* . . . There had been no more
storms. Would they come? If so, when? She
listened intently to the weather forecast each
evening but there were no predictions of
trouble. Everything was quiet.

For now . . .

At last Tamzin decided that she had had
enough. She just *couldn't* go on like this; it
was too much. Nothing terrible had happened
to her – she had to hold on to that, believe in
it, or she would go crazy.

By Friday evening she really had begun to
believe, and she was feeling much better. She
spent almost every waking hour of the weekend with Joel and the horses, working for her
riding lessons. She had learned to rise to the
trot now, and on Saturday afternoon Joel
started teaching her to canter. Cantering was
very different to trotting. As well as being

faster it was also a much smoother motion, a
bit like being on a rocking-horse.

'All you have to do is sit there, really,' said
Joel as they shortened their reins ready for
Tamzin's first try. 'Hold on to the saddle
pommel for a bit if you want to, till you get
used to it. And remember: heels down, knees
in, back straight!'

Tamzin grinned at him. 'I'll be as good as
you one day. Then we can have a race!'

'You'll have to learn to gallop first.' Joel
returned the grin. 'That's something! But you
know that already, don't you? After that
first time.'

Tamzin's face clouded as she remembered
how Moonlight had bolted with her on the
beach, and she resisted a sudden, strange
urge to look over her shoulder. It was foolish,
but she couldn't stop the momentary feeling
that something invisible was listening to her
and silently laughing. She had tried to put
the Grey Horse out of her mind. Now,

though, the familiar fear came creeping
back.

She said quickly, and perhaps a bit sharply,
'Yes, well, that was different. Next time, I'll
do it properly.'

Joel seemed puzzled by the change in her
tone, and just then a small cloud scudded
across the sun and a wing of shadow passed
over them. It made Tamzin feel cold. She
looked away, hoping Joel would say
something to break the tension. But he didn't.
Then the cloud moved on, and the sun came
back. *I'm not afraid*, Tamzin told herself.
I'm not. I'm not.

She blinked, looked at Joel again and with
a great effort made herself smile. 'Come on,'
she said. 'Let's get on with my lesson.'

On Monday, Mrs Beck had an announcement
to make. Every year the school held a Christmas fair, and each class made paintings and
crafts to sell for a charity chosen by the pupils.

This year, Tamzin's class was raising funds for an animal sanctuary, and that was to be the theme for their creations.

'We can have all kinds of animals, of course,' Mrs Beck said. 'But it would be great to concentrate on all the different creatures that live in Cornwall. So how about some ideas?'

Several of the class, including Tamzin, called out at once, 'Can we have horses?'

'Yes, of course we can,' said Mrs Beck. She smiled at Tamzin. 'Your nan paints horses, doesn't she? So how about you doing us some horse pictures to sell?'

'I can't really draw,' Tamzin said uncertainly.

'Well, maybe your nan would help you?' suggested Mrs Beck. 'You could ask her, anyway.'

A girl called Lisa, who was sitting next to Tamzin, said, 'What about lions?'

Tamzin looked at her in puzzlement. Mrs

* ★ ★

Beck was puzzled too. 'Lions?' she echoed. 'There aren't any lions in Cornwall!'

'There's one, Mrs Beck.' Lisa grinned mischievously. 'Lion Rock!'

Everyone groaned, and when the noise subsided Mrs Beck said, 'I get the joke! Very good. But I think we'll stick to real animals, all right? Come on, let's have some more ideas, and we'll make a list.'

As the rest of the class started to call out their suggestions, Lisa looked sidelong at Tamzin. 'Have you seen Lion Rock yet?' she asked.

'Yes,' said Tamzin. 'From the beach.'

'I've been right to it. In my uncle's boat. He took me out last summer, when the sea was calm. It's really creepy when you get close up, and much bigger than it looks from the shore.' Lisa smiled. 'He's going to take me again next year, with some friends. You can come, if you like.'

Before Tamzin could reply, Mrs Beck said,

'Lisa, there'll be plenty of time for that later, whatever it is. Come on, or you'll be the only one without an idea – and we want to win the prize for the most sales, don't we!'

Tamzin meant to talk to Nan about Mrs Beck's suggestion when she got home. But Nan was busy in her studio, and then it was tea time, and then Baggins bolted his food and was sick on the sitting-room carpet, and then there was a good programme on TV. So, with one thing and another, she hadn't got round to asking by bedtime.

She had an awful dream that night. She was running through the dark in a howling gale that roared and beat around her. Great gusts buffeted her from side to side, and the ground underfoot was rough and uneven, so that she stumbled and staggered and could hardly stay on her feet. She wanted to find somewhere to shelter and hide. But there was nowhere to hide, for the sea was rising up behind her, and she knew that if she did not run then it would come rushing over her and she would drown!

The wind screamed and roared, sounding like galloping hooves. Tamzin cried for help, but there was no one to help her. Then she heard a new sound, far behind but coming closer with every moment. Another kind of roar, deeper and steadier than the wind. The sea – it was overtaking her! She couldn't run fast enough, she couldn't escape! And the noise of the sea was like a deep, ugly voice, calling out over the wind's howl: '*GREY* . . . *GREY* . . . *GREY* . . .'

'Tamzin!' Someone was shaking her shoulder. 'Tamzin, wake up!'

The dream flashed away into nothing, and Tamzin jolted awake to find the light on and Nan at her bedside.

'You were having a bad dream, love,' said Nan. 'I heard you calling out, and you were thrashing around in bed. But the dream's gone now. You're awake and safe. Are you all right?'

Tamzin nodded. She felt shocked and breathless.

'Do you want to tell me about it?' Nan asked.

Tamzin hesitated, then shook her head. 'N . . . no thanks, Nan. I'd rather not.' She paused. 'What time is it?'

'Nearly two o'clock.'

Nan was still fully dressed. 'Hadn't you gone to bed?' Tamzin asked.

'No.' Nan sighed. 'I know it sounds silly, but I was trying to get that new horse painting right. I still can't make it work.'

'Mrs Beck was talking about your horse paintings at school today,' said Tamzin. 'We're having a Christmas art and craft sale for charity, and she asked if I could do a picture.'

'Did she?'

'Yes. But I can't draw. So Mrs Beck said to ask, would you help?'

* * *

Nan looked at her thoughtfully. 'Can't you draw?' she said. 'Have you ever really tried?'

Tamzin hadn't shown Nan the drawings she had tried to do of Moonlight. They weren't *that* bad . . . 'I suppose I haven't,' she admitted.

'Well, then.' Nan sat down on the bed. 'You wouldn't like to use my new picture to start you off, would you?' She gave a strange little laugh. 'I'm not getting anywhere; it doesn't seem to like me. Maybe it'll like you better.'

Tamzin's eyes widened. 'I couldn't, Nan! Your pictures are brilliant – I'd spoil it! Anyway, it'd be cheating.'

'No, it wouldn't. Mrs Beck did ask, after all. And you can tell her what you're doing.'

'But it's *yours*.' Tamzin couldn't explain, but the thought of painting on one of Nan's pictures, even if Nan encouraged it, felt all wrong and even a little bit frightening.

Nan, though, was looking at her keenly. 'Do you know,' she said, 'I don't think it is mine. It's just a feeling I've got, but . . . I think you're the one who *should* finish it.'

'Wh-what do you mean?' Tamzin asked.

'Remember when you came home from riding and found me having trouble with the painting? I first had the feeling then. I told you, didn't I, how I started painting blue horses because I hoped they were a . . . a sort of protecting influence. Well, maybe they are, or could be. But I don't believe it works for me; not any more. I've had my time, Tamzin. Now I think it might be your turn.'

Tamzin couldn't answer. She just stared, wide-eyed, and after a few seconds Nan smiled sadly. 'It was just an idea,' she said. 'I'm probably being silly. But think about it, and if you want to complete the picture . . .' She stood up. 'I suppose I ought to go to bed as it's so late. Will you be all right now, love?'

'Yes,' said Tamzin. 'I'm fine. Honestly.'

'Well, goodnight then.' Nan kissed Tamzin's cheek and left the room.

* ★ ★

For a few minutes there were sounds from
the bathroom, then came the click of Nan's
bedroom door closing. Tamzin knew she
should try to go back to sleep. But she was
afraid of having another nightmare, and
she was thinking about what Nan had said.
Nan *wanted* her to take over the troublesome picture. She truly believed it was the
right thing to do. So why was Tamzin afraid
to try?

She couldn't answer the question – or
perhaps she didn't want to. She turned over in
bed, picked up a book, and tried to
concentrate on reading.

That week at school Tamzin was in a dilemma
about Nan's picture. Mrs Beck had asked
again if Nan might help and Tamzin had told
a white lie, saying yes, well, maybe, and she
would ask. By Thursday, though, she was still
no nearer to making a decision.

Thursday was a blustery day, and by the

time Nan came to pick Tamzin up from school it was raining too.

'Typical October weather!' said Nan as Tamzin scrambled into the car out of the squally downpour. 'Never mind, the forecast says it'll clear up tomorrow so it shouldn't spoil your weekend for riding. The sea's huge; I walked to the beach to look. Full moon tomorrow too. There'll be big spring tides.'

Tamzin had learned about the spring tides, which happened at new and full moons. The sea came in and went out much further than at the neap tides in between. With any luck, she and Joel could canter all the way along the beach this weekend.

The wind boomed and the rain lashed round Chapel Cottage all evening, and Tamzin went to sleep with the noises in her ears. When she woke up it was nearly dawn, and she wondered what was different. Then she realized that the squalls had gone and the world outside was quiet and still.

She felt wide awake. And she was thinking, again, about Nan's picture.

She got up, pulled on a sweatshirt and padded quietly downstairs. The first dim light was creeping in at the windows, and Baggins greeted her with a sleepy meow from his favourite chair in the kitchen.

Tamzin went into Nan's studio. It was still too dark to see much, but the unfinished painting was just visible on its easel. She went up to it and peered.

The painting showed nothing but sea and sky. The horse Nan had begun to draw wasn't there any more.

Tamzin's heart bumped painfully. What had happened? Where was the horse? She ran to switch on the light, and as brightness flooded the room she hurried back to view the picture again.

One look, and she realized what an idiot she was. The horse's outline hadn't been spirited away by some awful, supernatural power.

Nan had simply painted over it; Tamzin
could see the new paint shining wetly where
it had been.

Suddenly she had an overwhelming impulse
to do what Nan had suggested and draw a
horse of her own on the painting. Nan used
charcoal, she knew, and there were some
sticks of it in a box on a nearby table. Tamzin
picked up a stick and stood squarely in front
of the picture. She imagined Moonlight
standing sideways on to the sea, his head high
and his mane and tail blowing in the wind. If
she could just capture that . . .

She reached out and made a bold, sweeping
stroke with the charcoal, as she had seen Nan
do. But she had forgotten about the wet paint.
Instead of the clear line she wanted, the
charcoal smeared in a huge, ugly grey smudge
over the picture.

Tamzin stared, horrified, at what she had
done. *Grey*, over the blue. In a single moment
all the terrors that she had tried to put out of

her mind came rushing and tumbling back. She had to clean the grey off! She mustn't leave it like this!

Snatching up a cloth she rubbed frantically at the charcoal smudge. But though a lot of it came off, some stayed, and spread further across the painting. It almost looked like a horse's shape.

Tamzin came close to panicking. There was only one other thing she could try, and she rummaged among Nan's tubes of paint until she found a blue that was about the same colour as the area she had spoiled. It took her nearly half an hour to cover up the charcoal smudges. But at last the grey could no longer be seen. Blue over grey. She had blotted out the dark influence. Nothing bad would happen. It wouldn't. It *couldn't*.

Feeling sick and frightened and horribly alone, Tamzin put the paint away, switched off the light and ran back upstairs to her room.

chapter ten

Despite Tamzin's fears, nothing dreadful happened that day. To her relief Mrs Beck didn't ask about the horse picture again, and she went home after school with the happier prospect of a weekend of riding ahead.

But that night, the bad dream came back. Again she was running through darkness with the wind raging around her and the sea roaring. This time, though, another sound was mingling with the racket of the storm – the sound of bells. They were ringing a wild peal, and to Tamzin's dream-locked mind the

* * *

clanging tones seemed to be saying, '*Blue, Blue! To you! Blue! Blue! To you!*'

Suddenly she snapped out of the nightmare and woke with a gasp. Her bedroom was dark but the sound of the bells was still going on. '*To . . . you . . . To . . . you . . .*' It was real, it was in the room . . .

Then Tamzin realized that her new mobile phone was ringing.

She grabbed the phone from her bedside table. 'H-hello?'

'Tamzin?' It was Joel. 'Sorry, but I had to call. There's something weird going on.'

Tamzin's heart started to beat faster. Joel's voice was strained, and all her nerve-ends tingled in response. 'What is it?' she whispered.

'I woke up a few minutes ago,' said Joel, 'and there were noises in the stable yard. When I looked out, I saw Moonlight. He'd got out of his stall somehow and he was escaping out of the yard, towards the valley. I think he's heading for your place. But that's not all. As he went through the gate, I . . . I . . .'

The tingle in Tamzin's nerves became as sharp as needles. 'What?' she asked.

There was a pause. Then, 'Tam, I know what I've said before. About the Blue and the Grey Horse being just a crazy old story. But I saw something in the yard. I didn't imagine it and I couldn't have mistaken it for anything else. It was another horse. A dark grey horse. It was as real as I am. It *looked* at me. But then suddenly it wasn't there any more.'

As he spoke the last words, Tamzin heard a rustle outside her window. She jumped violently and hissed into the phone, 'Joel, there's something in the garden, I just heard it! Wait a moment . . .'

It took all her courage to slip out of bed, cross to the window and pull back the curtain just enough to peep cautiously through.

Moonlight was in the garden. He was

* ★ *

wearing only a halter and she could clearly
see the frayed end of its broken rope dangling.
The pony raised his head, saw her and gave a
low, urgent whicker, pawing the ground
impatiently.

'It's Moonlight!' she hissed into the phone.
'He's here!'

'See if you can catch him,' said Joel,
sounding more strained than ever, 'and wait
for me. I'll be there in five minutes. And
Tam . . . I think I believe you now.'

He broke the connection. Moonlight
whickered again and stamped a forehoof
impatiently. He looked as if he would take off
at any moment, and hastily Tamzin dropped
the curtain and started to scrabble for her
clothes.

The house was dark and quiet as she felt
her way carefully downstairs. She wondered
if she should wake Nan, but instinct said no.
Joel was on his way; between them they could
cope with Moonlight.

* ★ *

Tamzin managed to ease the garden door
open without the squeaky hinges making too
much noise, and slipped outside. The night
air was chilly, and she shivered. The moon
was full and high in the sky, blotting out the
stars and giving a strange, silvery cast to
the garden and the valley beyond. It turned
Moonlight's coat to silver, too. He saw
Tamzin and came quickly towards her,
pushing his muzzle against her outstretched
hands.

'Moonlight!' Tamzin stroked him. 'There
now, it's all right! What are you doing here?
What do you want?'

The pony made small eager noises in his
throat. 'Shh!' Tamzin said. 'It's all right,
Moonlight, Joel's coming and – oh!'

Moonlight had jerked away from her, head
high and mane tossing. Tamzin made a frantic
grab for his halter rope and her fingers closed
round it just before he could snatch it from
her reach.

'Moonlight, no! Shh, now, what's the matter?' She tried to soothe the pony but he snorted and stamped, and when she pulled on the rope he pulled too, nearly dragging her off her feet. It was all she could do to hold on as they performed a strange, silent dance around the garden. Twice Moonlight almost broke free, and Tamzin was on the verge of giving up and shouting for Nan when footsteps thudded on the track beyond the garden and Joel arrived.

'Quick!' she whisper-shouted. 'I can't hold him!'

Joel came running, and between them they managed to get Moonlight under control. The pony was sweating; he stamped again and Tamzin jumped back, her feet only just getting out of the way of his hoof in time.

'Whatever's wrong with him?' she asked breathlessly.

'I don't know.' Joel was puffing with the effort of trying to calm Moonlight. 'He must

have come here for a reason but I've no idea
what it is. Moonlight! Moonlight, boy, what is
it? Stand still!'

Moonlight lowered his head, and it seemed
that he was going to obey. Joel's grip on the
rope relaxed – and in an instant Moonlight
had jerked it out of his grasp. The pony half
reared, turning on his haunches, and before
Tamzin or Joel could do anything at all, he
took off at a standing gallop. The low stone
wall surrounding the garden was nothing to
him; he rose like Pegasus, sailed right over it,
and was gone into the darkness.

Tamzin and Joel rushed for the gate and
piled through. 'Which way did he go, did you
see?' Joel gasped.

'Towards the beach, I think. Come on!'

Tamzin started to run. She pounded
round the curve of the track – and Joel nearly
cannoned into her as she stopped dead.

Moonlight was standing in the middle of the
path, facing them. A wind from the sea blew

his mane and tail like white smoke, and he let out a shrill whinny.

'Moonlight . . .' Tamzin took a slow pace towards the pony, holding out one hand.

'Careful,' Joel whispered. 'Don't excite him, or he'll bolt again.'

Moonlight didn't bolt. Instead, as Tamzin stepped forward he stepped back. He wasn't going to let himself be caught. But neither did he want to run away.

'Joel,' Tamzin whispered, 'he wants us to follow him.'

'That's crazy!' said Joel. 'He's only a horse; he can't reason like humans.'

'I think he can. And I don't think he's *only* a horse. Watch. I'll show you.'

She took another step towards the pony and said aloud, 'All right, Moonlight. I'm coming. I'm coming now.'

She began to walk along the path. For a second or two Moonlight watched her, then he turned and trotted on ahead. A few steps

* * *

and he stopped, looked back to be sure that Tamzin was still behind him, then moved on again.

'See?' Tamzin called to Joel.

Joel didn't argue any more. He caught her up at a run, and they both started to follow Moonlight along the path.

chapter eleven

The white pony led them at a trot on the uneven track. Joel had brought a torch, and the beam made a pool of light bobbing ahead of their feet and showing them the way. Tamzin's heart was thumping like a hammer. Once, she glanced over her shoulder. Back there was the safe haven of Chapel Cottage, while ahead lay mystery, the unknown; possibly even danger. Her sensible self said, *Don't do this – go home now and lock yourself indoors where it's warm and safe.* The desire to run away was powerful, but Tamzin fought it. She trusted Moonlight, and Joel was with her. Whatever was happening, wherever the pony was leading them, she had to see it through. Telling herself sternly that she must *not* look back again, she hurried on.

The cliffs rose up to their left, blotting out the moon, and suddenly the only light came from Joel's torch. They could no longer glimpse Moonlight, but they could hear the sea ahead of them, a deep, surging murmur in the night.

'We're almost at the beach,' Joel whispered.

Tamzin nodded, then remembered that he couldn't see her in the dark and said, 'Yes.' The ground was getting more uneven and they slowed down, mindful of the danger of twisted ankles. Then suddenly the valley opened out and they were at the beach.

The cliffs' black shadows stretched across the sand and made it invisible, but beyond the headlands the scene was lit again by the moon. The tide was far out, and the lines of breakers

showed white and ghostly against the pewter-
coloured sea.

Joel raised the torch. Moonlight was
illuminated in the beam like a phantom horse.
He was looking at them, waiting for them. As
they started to move again he disappeared
over the edge of the rough beach slope.

With the joggling torch to guide them they
slithered down the slope until their feet
ploughed into sand. Moonlight was a pale,
dim shape cantering towards the sea. He
reached the point where the headlands ended
and the beach widened out, then stopped,
and his shrill whinny carried back to them
on the wind.

Tamzin splashed through the shallow
stream that spread across the beach, running
to catch up with the pony. As she emerged
from the shadow of the headlands the moon's
cold white eye sailed out from behind the cliff,
bathing the scene in spectral light. The wind
was much stronger here, whipping her hair

back and blowing a fine mist of spume in her
face, and the sea's noise had grown to a
roar. It was like a voice calling to her with
a strange, wordless power. She stopped,
suddenly afraid, but Moonlight whinnied
again and came to meet her.

'Moonlight!' Tamzin hugged his neck,
feeling his warm breath on her face. 'What is
it? What do you want?'

Joel came hurrying up and took hold of
Moonlight's halter rope. This time Moonlight
didn't try to jerk away. Instead he pulled,
quite gently but with real determination.

'He still wants us to follow,' Joel said.
'Where, though?'

'I don't know,' said Tamzin. 'But we've got
to go with him.'

Moonlight tugged insistently on the rope
again, as if agreeing with her. Joel stared at the
sea and narrowed his eyes. 'The tide's turned.
It's coming in.'

'Maybe, but we've *got* to find out what

Moonlight wants!' Tamzin looked up and down the length of the beach, which stretched away into the vague distance. She admitted to herself that she was scared. Scared of the night and the thundering surf and the incoming tide. Yet she had come this far. She couldn't back out now. This mystery *had* to be solved.

'All right,' Joel said. 'We'll let him lead us a bit further, and see what he does.' He slackened the halter rope. 'Come on then, Moonlight. Show us.'

Moonlight immediately set off. Tamzin and Joel went with him, and at first they thought he was heading for the edge of the sea. But suddenly he veered off to the left, and Joel realized what he meant to do.

'He wants to go round the headland!' he said breathlessly. 'We can't let him. It's dangerous. We might get cut off by the tide!' He hauled on the rope, trying to stop the pony. 'Moonlight! Moonlight, whoa!'

Moonlight fought him, whinnying and

★ ★ ★

rearing, and Tamzin cried, 'Joel, let him
go! He knows what he's doing!' A huge,
suffocating sense of excitement was building
up in her. They were close to something, she
knew it – something vital!

Impulsively she made a grab for
Moonlight's rope and snatched it out of
Joel's hand. Joel shouted, 'Tam, don't!' But
Moonlight was already trotting away, and
Tamzin was running with him. For a second
Joel hesitated. Then he raced after them
towards the headland.

As if he knew that Tamzin could not run at his
speed, Moonlight kept his pace across the sand
to a trot. But Tamzin could feel his excitement. It was like an electric charge transmitted
through the halter rope. Whatever Moonlight
wanted her to see, it was very close.

The pony passed the first cave but as they
drew level with the second he wheeled sharply
and pulled towards the yawning mouth. The

* * *

cave looked black and vast and menacing, and
Tamzin's own excitement was swamped by a
wave of fear. She tried to push it down, telling
herself that it was only a cave and darkness
couldn't hurt her. Moonlight was walking
now, and she laid a hand on his neck to give
herself courage.

They reached the entrance of the cave and
were just about to go inside when Joel caught
up with them. 'Tam!' He grabbed her arm.
'You can't go in there!'

Moonlight snorted angrily. Tamzin stared
at the cave's black interior and swallowed.
'I think I've got to,' she said, her voice
unsteady. 'Moonlight wants it. It's important.'

'Look at the tide!' Joel pointed towards
the sea's edge. 'It's coming in fast, there isn't
time!'

'There is,' Tamzin said stubbornly.
'Moonlight knows. He won't let me come to
any harm.' She flashed Joel a look that was
pleading and challenging at the same time.

'I've got to do it, Joel. I'm going to, whether
you come with me or not!'

Joel opened his mouth to argue again, then
realized that it would be no use. Tamzin was
determined, and nothing he could say would
stop her.

'All right.' He nodded sharply. 'But I'll wait
by the headland, where I can keep watch on
the sea. Here, take the torch. If the tide starts
getting too close I'll shout – and whatever
you're doing, stop it and come running!'

'I will,' she promised. She glanced at the sea.
It did look perilously close, and she suppressed
a shiver.

'Give me Moonlight's halter rope,' Joel
added. 'He'd better stay here with me. He's
overexcited, and you might not be able to
handle him on your own.' Tamzin hesitated,
but he didn't give her time to protest. 'Go *on*!'

Moonlight didn't want Tamzin to go alone.
He fussed and danced and fought, but Joel
had a strong grip on his halter and made him

* * *

stay. Tamzin took a few paces, then looked back at them both. Moonlight was staring after her, but Joel's face was in shadow. She took a deep breath and entered the cave.

The sound of the sea changed to a hollow echo as she moved deeper in. It was cold in here, a dank, clammy coldness that seemed to clutch at her bones. What was she supposed to do? She didn't like being in the cave alone, and was tempted to run back and ask Joel to bring Moonlight and come with her. But when she turned to look at the silver-grey beach she saw how close the tide was. It was better, safer, that Joel should stay outside, to keep watch. She had so little time . . .

She turned again and started to move the torch slowly from side to side, scanning the cave walls. At first the beam lit only the craggy, broken rock face, veined with dull colours. But as the light reached the back of the cave, it was echoed by a quick, bright flicker that wasn't made by the torch.

* * *

Tamzin's heart stopped, thumped, then started to beat very fast. Right at the back of the cave was a long fissure. Something was there. Something that glowed with a small light of its own.

She switched the torch off, to be sure. The glow was still there, and it showed a small object wedged in the fissure, about three metres up. From here Tamzin couldn't see what it was. But a powerful intuition told her that this was what Moonlight had wanted her to find.

She switched the torch on again and looked at the cave floor. There was a pool at the back of the cave but it didn't look too deep, and beyond it were rocks that she could scramble up. She should be able to reach the fissure quite easily.

She pulled off her shoes and socks, rolled up the legs of her jeans and waded cautiously into the pool. The water only came to her knees, but it was stunningly cold and her feet tingled as she climbed up on to the lowest rock. The glow was still there, but it seemed to be fading. No matter: she knew where the object was. All she had to do was reach it.

Tamzin searched around for a safe foothold. Climbing with the torch in her hand wasn't as easy as she had hoped, but she went slowly and carefully, and within a couple of minutes her head was on a level with the object. The glow around it had vanished altogether now, and a rock spur cast a shadow in the torch beam, so she couldn't see it clearly. But it looked like a piece of stone, smaller than her fist . . . and with a thrill she realized what it must be. The missing piece from the statue she had broken – part of the head of the Grey Horse, which would make the figure whole again! It must have been washed here when she threw it into the sea. And, somehow, Moonlight had *known*.

Here was the chance she had been so desperately hoping for – the chance to put

right all the wrong she had done. Tamzin took
a deep breath, steadying her nerves. Then she
reached out and her fingers closed round the
stone fragment. It was slippery, so that when
she tried to prise it from the crevice she found
it hard to get a grip. But after a few seconds of
scrabbling and wiggling, it came free. Tamzin
thrust it deep into a pocket of her jacket and
started to make her way back down the rocks.
She splashed through the pool again and
back on to firm sand.

She was about to reach into her pocket
to take a proper look at what she had found,
when something moved at the cave mouth.

Tamzin's head came up quickly . . . and
her whole body turned frost-cold as she saw
the dark shape that barred her way out of
the cave.

It was a horse. A huge, storm-grey horse,
standing with its legs firmly planted and
its ugly head lowered. Its mane was as tangled
as seaweed and its eyes glinted like steel, their

glaring gaze fixed on her face. A chill, eerie light flickered over it, and through the light – and through the ghostly bulk of its body – the beach and the incoming tide were dimly visible.

Tamzin couldn't move a muscle. She could only stand rooted, staring in horror, as the awful truth smashed into her mind.

The Grey Horse was not just a legend. It really existed. And she was face to face with it.

chapter twelve

Tamzin's mouth worked, opening and shutting in jerky spasms. She was struggling to scream out to Joel, but no sound would come. She was frozen, helpless, so terrified that she couldn't make any move at all.

The Grey Horse lowered its hideous head still further, and bared its teeth in a silent threat. She tried to drag her gaze away from its awful stare, but it held her hypnotized.

Tamzin felt her hand start to move of its own accord, reaching into her pocket, groping for the stone fragment she had prised from the

137

crevice. The monster wanted the stone. It was willing her to take it, to hold it out, to give it . . . Tamzin's brain screamed at her to resist. But the dreadful eyes were boring into her mind, her will was weakening, she couldn't fight . . .

Suddenly the Grey Horse opened its mouth, and a low, ugly sound grated from its throat. Panic hit Tamzin and snapped the hypnotic grip. She didn't pause to think; instinctively she flung herself forward, trying to rush and dodge past the Grey Horse before it could stop her.

She ran three steps before an invisible force bowled her back like a leaf in a storm. Her feet went from under her and she fell to the sandy floor of the cave, rolling over and over until she fetched up hard against a rock. Gasping, she sat up. The Grey Horse had not moved. It still glared at her, and Tamzin realized the truth. The Grey Horse wanted the piece of stone – but even if she gave it up, the

＊　＊　＊

Horse would not let her pass. It meant to keep
her here. And a wild look past the monster
showed her that the tide was much closer. In
just a few more minutes it would reach the
headland, cutting off her escape route.

'*Joel!*' With a huge effort of will Tamzin
found her voice and screamed with all the
strength she could summon. '*Joel, help!*
Help me!'

There was no answering shout from outside.
Where was Joel? Had he seen the Grey Horse,
did he have any idea what was happening?
He was supposed to keep watch – why hadn't
he come?

'*Joel!*' she cried again, but her cry was lost
in the sudden boom as a huge wave broke out
to sea. It was a rogue wave, rushing in far
faster and further than normal; white water
surged almost to the cave mouth. There was
no time left. She *had* to get out now or it
would be too late. She had to take the Grey
Horse by surprise. It was her only chance!

* * *

Tamzin drew a deep breath and tensed her muscles. Then she leaped to her feet and darted for the cave mouth.

The Grey Horse gave a shrill scream and reared high, its hooves flailing the air. Tamzin recoiled – and as she reeled back she heard the roar of another great wave. As if the Horse's dark power had summoned it, a wall of water came smashing and pounding through the entrance. It bowled Tamzin over and swept her towards the back of the cave. Spluttering and gasping she made a desperate grab for a projecting rock, but missed. Then the wave hit the back wall, and the enormous recoiling wash carried her back to the entrance. She had one blurred glimpse of the rearing Grey Horse, then she was sucked out of the cave and into the full force of the waves.

The next few seconds were a terrifying roller-coaster of black darkness and silver water as Tamzin was hurled around in the thundering sea. She struggled to swim, but the

waves were far too powerful. Then another
great wave broke over her. It picked her up
as if she were a cork and hurled her towards
the shore. She was flung on to the sand and
the undertow swept back, leaving her high
and dry. She coughed and gasped and wanted
only to lie still until the banging in her head
went away. But there was no time. She had
to escape!

Tamzin staggered upright, started at a
stumbling run towards the headland – and
saw that it was too late. Waves were already
breaking around the headland rocks. She was
cut off.

As she slithered to a halt an eerie howl rang
out over the sea's noise. Tamzin looked wildly
over her shoulder and was in time to see the
Grey Horse emerge from the cave into the
glare of the moon. It galloped to the sea's
edge, and as it galloped its shape changed. It
was becoming part of the sea and, as it merged
with the water, a huge grey-crested wave

* * *

began to rise in the distance and sweep
towards the beach.

Tamzin's wail of terror was lost among
the noise of the sea, but this time her cry was
answered by a shrill, piercing whinny. She
whirled and saw another horse coming
towards her from the headland, plunging
through the battering waves. For a stunning
instant its coat looked blue – but then she
realized it was just a trick of the darkness,
and the truth hit her.

'*Moonlight!*' She stumbled across the sand
as the white pony sprang clear of the sea
and came galloping towards her. He skidded
to a stop; she grasped at his mane, hooked
an arm over his withers and with a frantic
kick hauled herself astride his back. Moonlight turned and, with Tamzin clinging on
for her life, he raced back towards the
headland.

The grey-crested wave crashed on the spot
where she had been standing, hurling up a

fountain of spray. But Moonlight was already clear. He charged into the sea again, and in seconds was swimming. Water slapped and surged and tried to wash Tamzin off, but she locked her arms around Moonlight's neck and, somehow, held on.

She could never have swum out beyond the rocks against that tide, but Moonlight was far stronger. Striking out powerfully, he cleared the headland and turned, almost surfing the breakers towards the beach. Suddenly he lurched as he felt sand under his feet, and moments later he was splashing out of the sea and cantering up the beach to safety. Only when he was well away from the sea did he slow to a trot. A figure came racing towards them from the direction of the beach slope, and through the pounding in her head Tamzin heard Joel's voice shouting.

'*Tamzin!*' He caught her as Moonlight stopped and she half slid, half fell from the pony's back. Hugging her tightly, he gasped,

* * *

'Thank God you're safe! I thought . . . I thought . . .'

'M-Moonlight saved me,' Tamzin whispered, trying to stop her teeth from chattering. 'I was cut off, and . . .' A huge shiver racked her.

'I know,' said Joel. 'The tide came in so fast, I couldn't get round the headland to warn you. Then Moonlight went crazy. He broke away from me and went after you.' He swallowed. 'I was running to get help when I saw him coming through the surf with you. Oh, Tam . . .'

He was staring towards the sea as he hugged her. But when Tamzin looked at his face, she saw that he wasn't taking in the scene. His eyes were frightened and bewildered, almost blank . . .

She managed the ghost of a smile and said huskily, 'I'm all right now. I am, really.'

Joel snapped out of his trance and back to earth. 'You're soaked through,' he said

144

worriedly. 'You must be freezing! Quick, take your wet jacket off. You can have mine.'

Tamzin pulled off her coat. She was about to drop it on the sand when Moonlight snorted and stamped. He thrust his head forward, pushing at one of the coat pockets – and with a jolt Tamzin remembered the stone she had found in the cave. The stone the Grey Horse had tried to make her give up. Slowly she reached for it and drew it out. They were just outside the cliff's shadow, and as she opened her hand the moon shone on the fragment.

Dismay filled her as she saw that it was not part of the head of the Grey Horse statue, but just a little bit of ordinary rock. Apart from the fact that it was covered in barnacles, there was nothing remarkable about it.

Or was there? Somewhere among the barnacles was a glimmer of blue . . . Tamzin's pulse raced. Hastily she scraped some of the barnacles away.

The stone broke into several pieces, revealing something else inside. Worn smooth as a pebble by the sea, it was a piece of glass, shaped in a graceful curve. And its colour was a deep, shimmering sapphire blue.

'Here's my jacket,' Joel said. 'And my fleece. Put them on.' He frowned. 'What have you got there?'

She turned to face him. 'I found a stone in the cave,' she said. 'I brought it back, and when I took it out of my pocket just now it broke open.' She held out her hand. 'This was inside. I think it's what Moonlight wanted me to find.'

Moonlight whickered softly, as though agreeing. Joel stared at the blue glass fragment, then gave a low whistle. 'That's spooky . . .' He reached out quickly, then drew his hand back, as if he were afraid to touch it. 'You'd better keep it safe.'

'I will,' Tamzin replied quietly. She tucked the glass carefully into the pocket of her jeans,

* * *

then put on Joel's fleece and jacket. She was
starting to shiver but it was only the cold now,
nothing worse.

'Come on,' said Joel. 'Better get you home
to get dry. I don't know what we're going to
say to your nan.'

That was the last thing on Tamzin's mind.
Anyway, she thought, Nan of all people would
surely understand.

They turned to go, then Joel said, 'Tam, the
blue glass . . . What Moonlight did . . . It's
important somehow, isn't it? But what does it
mean?'

Tamzin looked back at the sea and the
great crag of the headland. There were no
grey-crested waves, and no trace of the Grey
Horse. It had gone, at least for now. Would it
come back? Tamzin didn't know. But she
believed that another, kinder spirit was helping her to fight the Grey Horse, and tonight
it had used Moonlight to guide her to the
glass pebble. The pebble was a talisman. It

told her that the Blue Horse was out there somewhere, and if she could only find it, then she could put right the terrible mistake she had made, and defeat the Grey Horse's dark power.

In her heart she felt that she *would* encounter the Grey Horse again. It was a part of her family's history, and she knew now what Nan had really meant when she had said, 'It's your turn.' It was a frightening thought. But now, she had a little of the Blue Horse's strength to protect her.

Joel held her hand and squeezed it. She hadn't answered his question, but he knew she would tell him what she could, in time. Whatever the future held, he and Moonlight would be there. Together, they could win through.

And the Blue Horse was waiting for them. Somewhere.

Psst!
What's happening?

sneakpreviews@puffin

For all the inside information on the hottest new books,

click on the Puffin

www.puffin.co.uk

hotnews@puffin

Hot off the press!
You'll find all the latest exclusive Puffin news here

Where's it happening?
Check out our author tours and events programme

Best-sellers
What's hot and what's not? Find out in our charts

E-mail updates
Sign up to receive all the latest news
straight to your e-mail box

Links to the coolest sites
Get connected to all the best author web sites

Book of the Month
Check out our recommended reads

www.puffin.co.uk

Read more in Puffin

For complete information about books available from Puffin – and Penguin – and how to
order them, contact us at the appropriate address below. Please note that for copyright
reasons the selection of books varies from country to country.

www.puffin.co.uk

In the United Kingdom: Please write to Dept EP, Penguin Books Ltd,
Bath Road, Harmondsworth, West Drayton, Middlesex UB7 ODA

In the United States: Please write to Penguin Putnam Inc., P.O. Box 12289,
Dept B, Newark, New Jersey 07101–5289 or call 1–800–788–6262

In Canada: Please write to Penguin Books Canada Ltd,
10 Alcorn Avenue, Suite 300, Toronto, Ontario M4V 3B2

In Australia: Please write to Penguin Books Australia Ltd,
P.O. Box 257, Ringwood, Victoria 3134

In New Zealand: Please write to Penguin Books (NZ) Ltd,
Private Bag 102902, North Shore Mail Centre, Auckland 10

In India: Please write to Penguin Books India Pvt Ltd,
11 Panscheel Shopping Centre, Panscheel Park, New Delhi 110 017

In the Netherlands: Please write to Penguin Books Netherlands bv,
Postbus 3507, NL–1001 AH Amsterdam

In Germany: Please write to Penguin Books Deutschland GmbH,
Metzlerstrasse 26, 60594 Frankfurt am Main

In Spain: Please write to Penguin Books S. A., Bravo Murillo 19,
1° B, 28015 Madrid

In Italy: Please write to Penguin Italia s.r.l.,
Via Felice Casati 20, I–20124 Milano

In France: Please write to Penguin France S. A.,
17 rue Lejeune, F–31000 Toulouse

In Japan: Please write to Penguin Books Japan, Ishikiribashi Building,
2–5–4, Suido, Bunkyo-ku, Tokyo 112

In South Africa: Please write to Longman Penguin Southern Africa (Pty) Ltd,
Private Bag X08, Bertsham 2013